The Blood Waltz

The Blood Waltz

Ria Dimitra

Writers Club Press
San Jose New York Lincoln Shanghai

The Blood Waltz

Writers Club Press
an imprint of iUniverse.com, Inc.

For information address:
iUniverse.com, Inc.
620 North 48th Street, Suite 201
Lincoln, NE 68504-3467
www.iuniverse.com

ISBN: 0-595-12563-8

Printed in the United States of America

For M.W.

Contents

Chapter One

The Invitation

"Selena, you're not like other people."

That's what my mother used to tell me when I was younger. I was never certain if that was meant to be good or bad; I suppose that depended upon the context in which it was used. Frequently it was said during a heated discussion about how the *other* kids at school had this or were allowed to do that, so why wasn't I? But despite my constant efforts to fit in when I was younger, down inside, I knew I *was* different. Perhaps it was because I wrote my first full-length novel and began submitting it to various publishers around the country when I was fourteen; perhaps because on my tenth Halloween, when other little girls my age dressed as gypsies or witches or princesses, I went trick-or-treating as an Aztec priestess. (And may I stress that no one knew what I was. *No* one.) At any rate, I never led a normal life, so I suppose I shouldn't have been too surprised at the strange turn of events that changed me forever not too long ago. If it were to happen to anyone, naturally it would have to happen to me.

I had made regular visits to my mother's grave since she had succumbed to breast cancer nine years ago. Cemeteries give me the creeps—I've always had a hard time dealing with death—and I would only go there when it was bright and sunny. Still, something about the graveyard, with its silent tombstones and stone angels standing watch over its charges, chilled me to the center of my being. I couldn't stand the thought of my mother in such a place.

I would bring her flowers—yellow roses and purple irises were her favorites—and I would sit by her grave and tell her about the book I was working on, or the latest shenanigans of my cat Rufus, or how I had listened to *The Nutcracker* the day before and thought of her and of the times we used to listen to it together when I was small.

It was four years after my mother's death that I finally had a novel published—I was nearly twenty-three when my then-newfound agent Anne placed *Spraypaint and Glitter* with Pinecone Press. It was a novel for teenagers—or "young adults," as the publishing industry prefers to call them—about a teenaged boy who aspires to follow in the footsteps of his ne'er-do-well father, and finds out that all the actions of our heroes are not really worth imitating. It was followed by a plethora of other young adult novels on various themes—first love, fitting in, suicide, divorcing parents, you name it. I was churning out three or four of them a year, and my reputation—not to mention my audience—was growing. But then something happened. My last two novels were panned by the critics, and sales weren't nearly as high as expected. I even got some disappointed letters from fans. What had happened? Had my well of ideas run dry? Was I, at twenty-eight, losing touch with my readers?

"You're working too hard," Anne told me over the phone.

"What do you mean?" I asked. "I only wrote three books last year."

"'Only'? Selena, most people *never* write three books in a year. Maybe in their entire *lives*."

"It's not that hard when they're only about a hundred and fifty pages apiece."

"Selena, you're a remarkable person. You already have ten books on the market—"

"Eleven."

"*Eleven.* Sorry. *Eleven* books on the market, and you're not even thirty. Your fans love you, you're talented, you come up with all these great characters, your dialogue just zips along like a ride at Disneyland...but..."

"But what?"

I could hear Anne sigh audibly on the other end. "I don't know how to say this."

"Is it that bad?'

"Selena...you know as well as I do that your last two books were...well...not...not on the level of your earlier work."

"Oh, *that's* it. I'm losing my touch. I'm washed up. A has-been. My career is over before age thirty. So much for my fifteen minutes of fame. I guess I'll have to go back to answering phones."

"Selena, *no*, wait, that's *not* what I meant. What I mean is—maybe you're actually *tired* of young adult fiction. Maybe you should write something else for a change."

"Like what? I wouldn't know where to begin."

"Exactly. You've worked yourself into a rut. Selena, read my lips—*take a vacation.*"

"A vacation?"

"Yes, that's one of those things where you go somewhere far away and lie around and do nothing, in between visiting new places and going shopping."

"I *know* what a vacation *is.*"

"But you haven't *had* one since you've had me for an agent. You can't possibly, the way you keep sending me manuscripts thick and fast. You're working yourself to death—you're burnt out. Selena, if anyone needs a vacation, it's you."

"I...I don't know where...or how..."

"Call a travel agent. Talk to your friends. Go to the Bahamas or Aruba or someplace. Just get out of Atlanta for a while and forget that you're a writer. *Relax*, Selena. Then you can come back to work refreshed."

After I had hung up the phone, my mind was in a whirl. A vacation sounded good. There were so many exotic places I wanted to visit, I didn't know where to begin. I decided to talk it over with my best friend, Valerie Nicks, that evening.

"Am I invited?" Valerie asked with a glint in her eye as she twirled—or, rather, *tried* to twirl—some spaghetti around her fork. We sat cross-legged on my living room floor, eating on the coffee table, since my dining table was buried under piles of paper.

"Sure, if you want to come."

Valerie dropped her fork and pursed her lips as she knit her brow in a funny little grimace she always affected when she was irked that someone couldn't tell she was teasing. "Sel! You *know* I can't get off work! Cripes!" Valerie's attention left her plate just long enough for my large furball of a Siberian cat to swipe a piece of sausage off it and race for the kitchen. "Hey! Come back here! Sel, your cat stole my food!"

I couldn't help laughing.

Valerie returned her attention to snaring some more spaghetti. "Anyway, you probably *should* go by yourself. Who else would want to take care of your spoiled rotten cat while you're gone? Who knows," she added, as though a sudden thought had just struck her, "maybe you'll meet someone." She wiggled her eyebrows.

"Val, the man of my dreams does not *exist*, so I'm not going to meet him, on vacation or anywhere else."

"You're such a pessimist. It's a wonder any of your stories ever have happy endings."

"I live vicariously through my characters. They have the boyfriends, the good times, the popularity, the good looks I never had."

"Selena Marie D'Agostino! I swear!" Valerie threw her hands in the air. "You get letters from people you don't even know! Adoring letters from *guys* who want to *marry* you!"

"A sixteen-year-old boy who saw my *picture* on the back of one of his *sister's* books! That's not even *funny!*"

Valerie burst out laughing. "Okay, but Sel, you have to give yourself some credit. I don't even want to be *seen* with you. Guys never see *me* because they're always looking at *you*—especially when you wear those little blue Spandex pants under your sweater! I could strangle you!"

"My legs are the *only* good part of my anatomy. And anyway, you wouldn't *want* the guys who ask me out. I get all the weirdos. For some reason, I attract them like a magnet."

"Well, why don't you go to Egypt? Or maybe Mexico?"

I shrugged. "I don't know. I'd kind of like to go someplace where I speak the language. If I'm supposed to be relaxing, it's probably not a real good idea to get myself all stressed out trying to learn a new language. And who says I have to leave the country? I've never been out west. Maybe New Mexico or Arizona..."

By the time Valerie went back home to her apartment downstairs, I had a few ideas but still nothing concrete. I was going to try a travel agency the next day, but I slept in late, and as Fate would have it, the mail came early.

I was surprised to find an airmail envelope in the pile, amidst the junk mail and bills. I looked at the postmark: Wittcombe, U.K. I'd never heard of it. Overcome with curiosity, I tore the envelope open, wondering who could possibly be writing me from England. The letter inside was on very thin, slightly yellowy paper, and written in a large, flowery hand.

My dear Selena D'Agostino,

I hope this letter finds you in good health.

I am pleased to inform you that you are a descendant of James de Montfort, who built Castle Cormoran, near the town of Wittcombe, U.K., in the twelfth century. I have been tracing our family tree, back as far as the thirteenth century and forward to the present, and you are the only surviving member I have been able to locate outside of our little family that still remains here at Cormoran. Your ancestor, William Ramsey, emigrated to the United States in the eighteenth century, so we are very distant cousins.

I would like to extend an invitation to you to come visit us here at Castle Cormoran. You are welcome to stay as long as you wish. I look forward to meeting you, as do my son and nephew, who are my only surviving relations here in Britain. Please let me know when you would wish to come. I look forward to hearing from you.

Most sincerely yours,

Eugenia de Montfort

I read the letter twice, just to make sure I had really understood it the first time. I had distant relations who lived in an English castle, and they wanted me to come visit them. This was weird. *And* I had received this letter the *day* after Anne had told me to take a vacation. That was *weirder* than weird. I had known I was English on my mother's side, Irish/Italian on my father's; but I didn't know anything about my ancestors who had lived before my grandparents, and I hadn't been aware that my mother's family had been in the United States so long. Perhaps I was descended from aristocracy! Not that it would do me any good, but it would be personally fascinating. When I was a little girl, I had had daydreams of being a princess, or some sort of grand lady; now I was going to go meet my relatives at their castle.

That thought occurred to me without hesitation; it was never an option *not* to go. Of course I had to go. Eugenia de Montfort had traced nine centuries of our family's history, in what must have been a Herculean task, probably taking up most of the years of her life. I wondered how old she was, what she looked like. And her son and nephew—were they my age, older, younger? What were they like? Would there be any family resemblance, or were we so distantly related that they would be merely strangers?

I went to my bedroom closet and pulled out the old photo albums my mother had left me when she died. I'm not aware of any living relatives on her side; her family seemed to have a penchant for dying young. I used to call it "The Ramsey Curse," adding that since I was a D'Agostino and not a Ramsey, that I was immune. But that was to mask the fear that lurked down inside that I would be like my mother, dead at forty-four. I tried to push the fears aside as I opened the photograph albums.

Crumbling black paper pages held brownish photographs of faces I didn't know. Here and there the little black corners had come loose and photos had fallen out. Faded, squirrely old handwriting on the back of some of the photos gave a few cryptic clues: a year, a name that was meaningless—Susie and Jean, or Uncle Henry. I wasn't sure which people were actually my relatives and which were just family friends. I hoped to find out who all these people were. But more than that, I hoped to find myself.

***

My father hadn't sounded suitably impressed when I dropped by his house and told him I was going to England. He seemed to think the whole thing was a sham, someone who knew me from my books and was putting me on, probably trying to get something out of me.

"But, Dad, if she knew me just as an author, she would have addressed me as Selena *Young*, not Selena *D'Agostino*. *And* she knew Mom's maiden name. Besides, I've been very careful about keeping my home address private. It was addressed directly to *me*, it hadn't been forwarded from my agent or my publisher or anyplace. I think it's for real."

"So you go and meet these people. Then what? Are they going to leave you a big inheritance or something? I think not."

"Dad, I don't want anything. I just think it would be cool to find out about my roots. Besides, everybody's telling me to take a vacation, and then *this* falls into my lap. It's like an omen."

"Yeah, well, suit yourself." He busied himself with polishing his glasses.

"Dad, what do you know about Mom's family?" I asked softly.

My father looked up at me, an unreadable look on his face. "Not much."

"Tell me what you know."

He shrugged. "They were an old English family that came over before the Revolutionary War. Rather uppity, if you ask me." He went back to polishing his glasses.

"You never cared much for Mom's family, did you?"

"The feeling was mutual." He put his glasses back on. "We just came from different worlds, your mother's family and I."

"That's why we didn't visit them much, isn't it?"

"They didn't think I was good enough for Kathryn. They never forgave her for marrying me."

"And that's why you don't want me to go."

"No, that's not why. I just don't want to see you get hurt."

"I'm not going to get hurt. And anyway, Mom's British relatives may not be anything like her American relatives. But they're my relatives, too, Dad."

"Selena, you're a big girl. I'm not going to tell you what to do. Be careful."

At least Valerie was more enthusiastic. I went downstairs to tell her as soon as I heard her come home from work.

"You have relatives who live in a *castle*? Sel, now I *know* you are not like other people."

I laughed. "Who'd have thought?"

"*I* would. Now, why hadn't *I* thought of that—England is probably a great place to meet guys. I mean, they're so charming and polite—and they have the greatest accents."

I rolled my eyes. "Val, they live near some town called 'Wittcombe.' I looked for it in my atlas—it's not even on the map! It probably has a population of about fifty people, probably all old-timers who used to fish out of little dinghies with a net."

"It's near the sea?"

"I have no idea where it is."

"Well, I think you should go. Like you said, it's obviously an omen. A quiet, out-of-the-way place may be just what you need. Plenty of R and R. You could make a side trip to London, as long as you're over there. Do some excellent shopping."

"Yeah, that's a good idea. I'm going to write Eugenia and tell her I'm coming."

***

The next few weeks were spent in preparation. I wrote Eugenia immediately to accept her invitation and set to work applying for my passport and booking my flight to London. I decided to go to Castle Cormoran first, saving London for last—I felt that I needed the quiet and relaxation first. Besides, I couldn't wait to meet my relatives. What would they be like?

Eugenia wrote me again, saying how thrilled she was that I was coming, and instructing me on how to get to Wittcombe from London's Gatwick Airport. No trains ran through the town, so I was told to go as far as Leeds, where, I was informed, someone would fetch me and take me the rest of the way to Castle Cormoran by automobile. No clue was given as to whom this "someone" might be.

Valerie was to drive me to the airport. I got up early and rushed around to get ready, making certain I didn't forget anything. On one last trip to the bathroom, as I was washing my hands, I looked up and caught my reflection in the mirror. Would Eugenia and her son and nephew look anything like me? Like my mother? My heart began to pound as, for the first time since I had gotten Eugenia's first letter, I began to get nervous.

"Come on, Sel, let's go!" Valerie yelled as she banged on my door. I quickly dried my hands and went to gather up my bags.

"Don't forget to feed Rufus and clean out his litterbox," I reminded her on the way to the airport. "And get my mail. And water my plants."

"Yeah, yeah, I know, I know."

"I'm sorry. I'm just nervous."

Valerie cast me a sympathetic glance. "It's gonna be *fun*."

"I've never left the country before. What if I get lost?"

"You won't get lost. Someone's going to pick you up in—where?"

"Leeds."

"Yeah."

"But I could get lost before I get as far as Leeds."

"You're such a worrywart. Loosen up."

Valerie saw me as far as the baggage check, where she gave me a hug and wished me luck. "Send me a postcard," she said.

"I will."

"Take care of yourself. I'm expecting to see a change in you when you come back!"

How I wish now she could take back those words.

Chapter Two

The Meeting

I sat on the airplane listening to Tchaikovsky on my Walkman, closing my eyes and trying to imagine what Castle Cormoran might look like. I dreamed of its having several towers rising majestically into the sky, surrounded by a moat and set in the gently rolling hills of the English countryside. Anne had told me to "forget I was a writer" while I was on vacation, but I had stashed a thick notebook and a number of pens in my suitcase, just in case I was struck by a sudden inspiration for a story. Who knows—perhaps a castle was the perfect setting for an historical romance. I had also taken care to pack my camera and plenty of film.

My first impression of England was *green*; from the air, the fields below were of an uncommonly green hue that I had never seen before back home. It was the beginning of April, so I would be just in time for spring, I reasoned; and what could be more peaceful and conducive to relaxation than springtime in the English countryside?

Gatwick Airport was bustling but not maddeningly overcrowded, and I had no difficulty getting my bags and checking through Customs.

The man who checked my passport cheerily asked, “Here on holiday?” as he stamped it.

“Yes,” I said, without missing a beat. I had boned up on my “British English” in preparation for my trip, not wanting to appear to my British relations—or any other Englishmen I encountered—as a total moron. “I’m here to meet some distant relatives.”

“In London?”

“No, Castle Cormoran.” The man looked blank. “It’s near Wittcombe.” Still blank. “North, I think.”

He smiled, though I could tell he’d never heard of the place. “Enjoy your stay. Good day.”

I had a strange feeling as I walked away from Customs and headed for the train. This man worked at the second-largest airport in what was actually a rather small country, and he had never heard of the place I was going. I remembered the remark I had made in jest to Valerie about the likelihood of Wittcombe’s not having more than fifty inhabitants, and wondered whether perhaps I had the hit the nail on the head. It had to be a small, out-of-the-way place.

The train ride to Leeds was long, my butt was sore and my legs were cramped from the long airplane ride, but I scarcely minded as I watched the scenery go by. The houses seemed quaint, old-fashioned; everything had a different *look* to it; proof, I suppose, that I was in a different country from the one I was used to. Everything looked more *European*—yes, that had to be it.

My heart pounded in anticipation as the train rolled into the station at Leeds. Who would be meeting me here? And how would I know him—or her? I buttoned up my black raincoat with the zip-out quilted lining—an item which no one either living in or visiting England should be without—and disembarked. It was chilly out, colder than it had been when I left Atlanta. It didn’t take long to figure out who was there to pick me up: a somber-faced man in a long black coat stood several feet away, holding a large white placard that said “Selena

D'Agostino" in bold black letters. I was mortified. He might as well have had a red light flashing on top of his head and a siren. I quickly walked up to him, hoping he would put that damned thing away.

"I'm Selena D'Agostino," I said quickly, my voice low. I showed him my passport. He nodded and gestured for me to follow him. "And you are—?" I ventured as I fell into step beside him.

The man shook his head.

"Are you Eugenia's son?" I pressed.

He shook his head again.

"Her nephew?"

Another shake. What was his problem? I was getting irritated. Just then, he signed something with his hands, but I had no idea what it meant. *Great—my first contact with the de Montfort family, and he's mute.*

The mute man opened the back door of a large, black, old but expensive-looking car for me and then threw my bags into the trunk. Needless to say, the drive to Castle Cormoran was made in silence. I was frustrated, because I had hoped to find out a few facts about the place before I got there. We drove through the town of Wittcombe, a tiny hamlet that looked as though it were still in the Middle Ages, with its timber and stucco buildings. The only anachronism was the occasional car or bicycle, and the television antennae on the roofs. Dusk was falling, and there were few people on the streets; but those that were eyed the black car with glances that could only be construed as hostile, before quickly disappearing inside the buildings. I wondered whether perhaps the de Montforts were known and resented in the town for some reason.

My first glimpse of Castle Cormoran was forbidding, to say the least. As castles go, it wasn't gigantic; but its majestic austerity, rising atop a hill and set against a rapidly darkening sky, overwhelmed me. Twin towers flanked a wide, arched doorway that served as the castle's main entrance. The grounds had fallen into a state of disrepair, with weeds poking up between the cobblestones of the drive and choking off the grass. A pair of peafowl ambled proudly across the lawn. My mental image of an airy, romantic castle—something along the lines of Camelot, perhaps—was rapidly being displaced by the stark reality of this dark, slightly ominous fortress. Were it not for the peacock and his mate, I would have found the place extremely gloomy.

The black Daimler slowly rolled over the drawbridge and through the gate to the inner ward, where the mute driver stopped and got out to assist me with my bags. He piled them on the crumbling cobblestones and got back into the car and drove away. I looked up at the massive stone walls that rose above me and shivered.

"Selena!" a clear, melodious voice called out. I spun around to see a slim woman with silvery hair, dressed in a black dress with a white lace collar, approaching me from the gatehouse with her arms extended. She smiled radiantly at me and reached for my hands. "Here you are at last! I've *so* looked forward to meeting you!"

"Eugenia?" I asked hesitantly.

"Please—do call me Aunt Eugenia. It would be a pleasure."

"Sure."

"Come in, do come in." She directed her attention to the mute driver, who had by this time returned from parking the car. "Derek, take Miss D'Agostino's bags to her room." She turned her attention back to me. "I'll show you to your room shortly. First we must get acquainted. Let's have some tea."

I followed Eugenia down a dim hallway lined with massive portraits in heavy, gilded frames. I wanted to stop and look more closely at the faces of what I knew, with a vague feeling of excitement, were my ancestors, but Eugenia was moving along at a good clip and I didn't want to lose her. There would be more time for ancestors later.

Eugenia led me up a winding spiral staircase to a parlor on the second floor furnished with faded Persian rugs and mismatched furniture, with styles spanning several centuries. A fire roared in the large stone fireplace, reflecting off the gilt trim of a large, black Oriental chest-on-chest.

Kerosene lamps flickered on the walls, and I wondered, with some consternation, whether the place had electricity—or running water, for that matter. A tea service was already waiting on a small occasional table in front of the fireplace, and Eugenia poured two cups.

"Sugar? Milk?"

"Yes, please—both." I had never had milk in my tea before, but I understood the British did, so I figured that perhaps the way to get off to a good start with my newfound relatives would be to try to fit in a little.

I sat down in one of the leather-upholstered chairs that flanked the small table. Eugenia handed me a steaming cup and sat down in the chair opposite me. She seemed to glow from every pore. I hadn't realized my visit meant so much to her. "I can't decide whom you look like," she said.

"I'm told I favor my father's side of the family."

"Oh, but I can tell there's some de Montfort in you, as well. It's in your complexion...your mouth...your hands."

I looked down at the hand holding my teacup. I had always had compliments on my hands. Someone had once told me they looked as though I'd never done a day's work in my life. Now I knew where they came from.

"Who was the man who drove me here?" I asked.

"Oh, that's Derek. He's worked for the family since he was fifteen."

"He's mute?"

"Yes, but he can hear. We have only a handful of servants these days—Derek; and then there's Sissy, our cook; and Ellen. We're hopelessly understaffed, I'm afraid."

I laughed. "I'm sure I can put up with it. Are your son and nephew the only other family members?"

"Yes, Philip—such a dear boy—and Kieran."

"Kier–?"

"Kieran. It's an old family name."

"It's...different. Are they around?"

"Oh, somewhere." Eugenia waved a hand in a dismissive gesture. "You'll meet them soon. They're not quite as social as I am." She laughed, a clear, delightful laugh that seemed to bubble up from her throat. "Please don't hold it against them. Do you ride?"

"I beg your pardon?"

"Horses. Can you ride a horse?"

I blanched. "The only horse I ever sat on was made of wood and had a pole through it."

Eugenia unleashed her bubbly laugh again. "I'm sure Philip would be happy to teach you. He's an excellent rider."

"I'm looking forward to it."

"I'm sure the lads will do whatever they can to make your stay as enjoyable as possible."

I was dying of curiosity to meet Philip and Kieran and wondered why they didn't seem as eager to meet me. Perhaps they were shy. I just hoped they weren't snobs.

"I'm looking forward to finding out about my family history," I said. "I know so little."

"You're lucky to have been born into such a colorful and noble family," Eugenia said, with obvious pride. "And fortunately, well-documented. The lads are well versed in history as well, so feel free to ask them whatever you wish. Kieran has a degree from Oxford."

He must be a brain, I thought. I hoped he wouldn't think his lowly American cousin to be an imbecile.

"So, what do you do for a living, my dear?"

"I'm a writer."

"Indeed? What do you write? Books?"

"Yes. Novels…for teenagers."

"Ah. Popular fiction?"

"I guess you could call it that."

"How fascinating. Did you bring any of your books with you?"

My face fell. I should have thought of that. "No, I...I'm afraid I didn't. I could mail you one when I get home...?"

"Oh, do. You must get your talent from us de Montforts. We've had a few writers amongst our ranks...as well as some painters and musicians." She smiled. "We're a very talented, intelligent family. Such a shame we seem to be dying out. You have no children?"

"No, I've never been married."

"Well, you're young, there's still time. And Philip and Kieran..." She shook her head, clucking her tongue. "Such fine, handsome lads...they've never married, either."

"Any special reason?" I asked. Gossiping about other people's marital or romantic states has always been one of my vices.

"I don't know. They're perfectionists, I suppose. And what about you? Any special man in your life?"

I laughed. "Oh, no. I've had nothing but disasters."

"What a pity. You're such a lovely girl, it's a shame your parents never had any more children. So pretty." She smiled fondly at me.

I squirmed uncomfortably. I'd heard the old "When are you going to give me grandchildren?" routine from my father more times than I cared to count. Being an only child placed the entire responsibility on my shoulders.

"Well, you'd probably like to go to your room to freshen up before dinner." Eugenia got to her feet. "Let me show you."

I followed Eugenia down another hall and up some more twisting stone steps to a bedroom—I think Eugenia called it a "chamber"—in a large tower. A large four-poster bed, surrounded by heavy, dark green draperies, which made it resemble a tent, dominated the room. The bed looked comfortable with its profusion of pillows and its thick velvet coverlet in shades of green, deep purple, and dusty rose. A couch covered in peach-coloured silk and strewn with still more pillows stood at the foot of the bed, and across from it a fire flickered in the stone fireplace, which was topped by a very large mirror in an ornate gilded frame. A wash basin and a large pitcher atop a heavy, carved chest of dark wood seemed to confirm my suspicions about running water.

"Uh...where can I take a bath?" I asked hesitantly. "And use the toilet?"

"There's a tub two doors down, and the water closet is next to that. Derek will be up in ten minutes to show you to the dining hall." Eugenia quietly withdrew.

I checked my reflection in the mirror, combed my hair, and then started down the hall to the "water closet." I knocked on the door and, when no one responded, slowly opened it. It was no bigger than a closet, all right, and all that was inside was a tiny, arched window and a stone slab with a hole in it. My brow wrinkled in consternation—I saw no handle or other flushing apparatus. There wasn't even any toilet paper. I walked over to the hole and peered in. It appeared to be just that—a hole. "Wait till Valerie gets a load of this," I mumbled.

Derek appeared at my door in exactly ten minutes to lead me downstairs and through the inner ward to the dining hall. He was so stony-faced, and even his movements seemed terribly stiff, that I could not imagine him talking even if he were able. He opened the door for me and disappeared.

The dining hall was a long, high-ceilinged room with a few long, narrow windows along one wall. Above each window was a smaller, more squarish window with a fearsome-looking dragon depicted in stained glass. A couple of very large, very faded, and very old-looking tapestries hung on the long wall that faced the windows; and the remaining wall space was cluttered with large, darkly painted portraits. A deer head with gigantic antlers hung over the large fireplace at one end of the room; and a long, heavy table of dark wood, flanked by at least twenty chairs with tall, carved backs, filled most of the room. Candles flickered in silver candelabra on the table, and at the end opposite the fireplace was a single place setting. I was puzzling over this as a stout woman with her blonde hair pulled back in a bun and wearing a white apron wheeled a cart of food into the room.

"Aren't the others eating?" I asked as she began loading up the table's single plate. She shook her head. "Eugenia, Philip…?" My voice trailed off as she shook her head again, gestured at the plate, and withdrew. *Not another mute servant*, I thought to myself. Well, Eugenia was obviously an equal opportunity employer. I thought it rather rude that my hosts wouldn't even eat with me. Surely they had to eat *sometime*. My growling stomach didn't care whether I had company or not, so I sat down and ate. The food did not live up to my expectations—it was rather bland—but it filled my stomach. The cook returned and tried to give me seconds, but I insisted that I was full and she removed the cart. When I had finished eating, I returned to the gatehouse through the inner ward, going back the way Derek had led me in, hoping I could find my way to my bedroom on my own. I didn't really want to go to bed already, but I decided daylight was a better time to explore the castle, and besides, everyone seemed to have disappeared.

I think I had become quite thoroughly lost somewhere on the second floor when the lilting strains of a violin caught my ear. I stopped to listen. Strauss, I thought to myself, but I couldn't recall the name of the piece. Whoever was playing it sounded masterful, certainly good enough to be playing in an orchestra. The music seemed to beckon to me, and I followed, determined to find its source. I found a door that was slightly ajar, and the music was becoming noticeably louder. I quietly entered the room, not really wanting to sneak up on whomever was there, but rather so that I might steal a glance before my presence was detected and the stiff mask of formality presented to me. A slender figure, obviously masculine, had his back to me and was dressed in a white shirt with full sleeves, snug black trousers, and black riding boots. A mane of long black hair fell more than halfway down his back, and he seemed to be of fairly average height—I had him pegged for about five foot nine. I was not aware that I had made any sound, but I had been standing there only a few seconds when he abruptly stopped playing, lowering his violin and spinning around, as though he had sensed I was there.

He was a very striking man, probably around my own age. The first thing I really noticed about him was his eyes—they were dark and fathomless and stared intensely at me, almost as though they might burn two holes through my body. The eyebrows above them were dark, though not heavy, and had a nice hint of an arch to them. He had a long, thin, immaculately clean-shaven face, with a long, aristocratic nose and a sensual mouth, the corners of which twitched upward slightly. I don't think I would go so far as to call it a smile; coupled with the look in his eyes, I think perhaps the expression qualified as a smirk.

"I didn't mean to intrude," I said quickly. "I just heard someone playing, and it sounded very beautiful, so I wanted to check it out." *What a stupid thing to say,* I told myself. *I sound like a total moron.*

The smirk deepened as he genteelly inclined his head. Rather than merely accepting my compliment to his musical talent, he seemed to be mocking me. I decided then and there that I was not going to let this man intimidate me. "Are you Philip?" I ventured.

He gave a brief snort and said, "No, I'm not Philip." His voice took me completely by surprise; although he had the cultured, uppercrust British accent that Eugenia had, it had a rough, raspy, throaty quality that provided a startling contrast to his elegant looks. He took a few steps closer to me, set down his bow, and extended a smooth, fair-skinned hand. "Kieran Ramsey."

I began to put forth my hand, with the intention of shaking his. "I'm—"

He cut me off. "Selena D'Agostino." I was surprised that he actually pronounced it correctly; most people butcher my last name, which is why I chose something simple like "Young" for my pen name. Instead of shaking my hand, he gently lifted it to his lips, studying me from the tops of his eyes. As he slowly lowered my hand, he said, "We've been expecting you."

I was so dazed by this display of gentlemanly chivalry that I was struck speechless, but only for a moment. "You and Philip are cousins?"

"Of a sort." Kieran slowly moved to a chair, setting his violin on top of a small table beside it and sitting down. He waved me to a chair facing him and I sat down carefully. He stretched out his legs, which seemed long for his height, crossing them at the ankles. His every movement seemed slow and deliberate, and I had the feeling that he was mentally sizing me up as he regarded me with those dark, unnerving eyes. The most maddening thing about it was, his expression gave no clue as to the verdict. "Philip is the golden boy of the family," Kieran said archly, "since he is a *de Montfort* and I am merely a *Ramsey*."

"What's wrong with that?" Being a middle-class American of mixed European ancestry, I've never understood any of this blue-blood snobbery. My parents have always stressed personal accomplishment over ancestral lineage.

Kieran gave me a look of bored tolerance, as though I were a simpleton and he were about to impart some great wisdom for my benefit. "The Ramsey side of the family—of which you and I are apparently the only survivors—is descended from a James Ramsey, who lived in the sixteenth to seventeenth centuries, and his Spanish mistress. She was a commoner, besides not being English, so we're considered a wee bit less *noble* than the *de Montforts*." He stressed this last word with what seemed to be distaste, and his eyebrows shot up for emphasis, making them arch even more than before.

I couldn't help smiling. "I've never considered myself a member of the nobility in the first place, so it makes no difference to me if I'm descended from someone's mistress, or whatever. I've got more foreigners and commoners in my past than any of you people."

"It's not just that," Kieran said, "he never did marry her." I got the feeling that he didn't like this topic, since he chose to change it by offering me a drink. Normally the only alcohol I consume is the occasional wine cooler, and I didn't think he was going to offer me one of those; but I didn't want to seem rude, so I accepted. As he got up from his chair and made his way to a sideboard by the wall, I thought to myself that I probably seemed dreadfully uncouth to this family. Well, I told myself, the worst that could happen would be that I might make a fool of myself and never be invited back again. How I wish now it could be so simple.

Kieran glanced back at me over his shoulder as he asked, "Will red wine be acceptable?"

"Uh, sure," I said feebly. He poured two glasses from a glass decanter and walked back to the chairs, handing me one before he sat down with the other. I took a small sip as Kieran watched me, probably to see if I would choke. In fact, I didn't *see* him watch me—I felt him. A glance over at him confirmed my suspicion—he was eyeing me over the rim of his glass before slowly taking a sip. My face grew hot. Did he have to *stare?*

"I understand you're a writer," he said.

This time I nearly did choke. "How did you know that?"

Kieran gave me a small, bemused smile. "Eugenia told me."

"What else did she tell you about me?"

He shrugged lazily. "Not much." I had the feeling he was toying with me. Well, two could play this little game—I wasn't going to make things easy for *him,* either.

"Eugenia told *me* some things about *you,* too," I said airily.

Kieran didn't seem very concerned. "I'm sure 'twas not any of the more *interesting* things."

"Such as what?" I blurted out before I could stop myself.

He gave me that smirky smile again and arched his eyebrows. "Perhaps you'll find out during your stay." It struck me all of a sudden that perhaps he was flirting with me; a lot could be read into the look in his eyes. I didn't say anything, and I could tell from the look on Kieran's face that he knew he was making me squirm and was enjoying every minute of it.

"So, what do you write?" he asked, after letting me suffer for a few minutes.

"Teenage novels."

"Indeed?" Only one eyebrow went up this time. "Romances?"

"Sometimes...to a degree."

"Do you write from personal experiences?" He put up a hand. "No, wait. Let me guess. 'Sometimes...to a degree.'"

My face flamed. "You don't have to make fun of me," I said, growing irked with him.

"My dear cousin...I'm not making fun of you. Perish the thought." He put his hand to his chest in a feigned display of wounded pride. "I'm only anticipating what you're going to say."

"Could I speak for myself, please?" I said, rather snidely.

Kieran inclined his head. "By all means."

"I didn't grow up in a convent."

"I didn't think you did." He gave me a wicked smile. "We haven't any saints in our family." He raised his glass. "To the Ramseys."

I raised my glass to his toast and slowly took a sip as I watched him down what remained in his glass in one gulp. He nearly slammed the glass onto the table beside him, making me jump. He got up and walked back to the sideboard for the decanter, which he brought back with him, refilling his glass. I was going to ask him why I had been left to eat dinner by myself, but the thought flew away, promptly forgotten, as I watched Kieran leisurely pour himself some more wine and then slowly look up at me, straight into my eyes. The corners of his mouth gently lifted once again, as though he had some private joke on his mind. Somehow, I had the feeling that the joke was on me.

"More wine?" he asked, reaching over with the decanter and pouring more into my glass before I could respond.

"Please—no. I have enough, thanks. Really."

Kieran's little smirk simply refused to go away. "Relax, cousin. You need to unwind." There was no escaping those eyes. I felt like some small, hapless animal being hypnotized by a snake, and my mind fluttered desperately for some escape.

"What were you playing when I walked in?" I asked nervously, abruptly changing the subject. "Strauss, wasn't it?"

Kieran nodded, obviously pleased that I possessed as least *some* knowledge. "'Tis the 'Vienna Blood Waltz.'"

"Oh, yeah. I knew it sounded familiar, but I couldn't remember the name. That's a very beautiful piece, and you play very well. I'm sorry I interrupted you—perhaps you'd play some more?"

Kieran smiled smugly, his ego obviously kicking into high gear. "With pleasure." He picked up his violin and his bow and rose to his feet. A sweet, soaring melody filled the room as he began to play, his body moving with it languidly as he closed his eyes and a look of serene pleasure settled on his face. I wondered to myself whether he were playing the thing or making love to it. He opened his eyes a little, watching me from beneath half-lowered lids, his mouth twisting into another coy little smirk. I wondered whether his playing, like his conversation, was meant to be taken on two levels.

I was spellbound by Kieran's prowess on the violin and sat listening to him for some time, unaware of the time that had passed. I must have finally yawned, because he stopped and asked me if I wished to "retire for the night" (his term). "I've kept you up too late," he said.

"Oh, that's all right," I said. "But I guess I should get to bed—if I can find my way back." I paused, but he made no comment. I was embarrassed to admit I'd gotten lost, but I figured I was going to have to, anyway. "Could you…could you please show me the way back to my room? I'm afraid I got…turned around."

I'm sure Kieran found this amusing, but to his credit, I have to say that at least he was a gentleman about it and didn't laugh at me—not out loud, anyway. "Certainly, dear cousin."

I thought it strange that he kept referring to me as "dear cousin" when we were so distantly related and had only just met. But I chose to ignore it. "Thank you."

Kieran led the way around a corner in the corridor and up some stairs, and I noticed he had a very light tread. But then, I reasoned, he couldn't have weighed more than a hundred and forty pounds, soaking wet. When we reached my room, he opened the door with a flourish, bowing as he swept an arm through the doorway. "Your chamber, m'lady," he said, inclining his head. I felt he was mocking me again, but something in his eyes made me promptly forget all my snappy comebacks. I felt slightly weak.

"What time is breakfast?" I asked.

"Whatever time you wish, dear cousin." Kieran put one hand on the doorhandle, and, before closing the door behind him, raised his eyebrows and lowered his voice as he said, "Pleasant dreams." I had a brief glimpse of a wicked smile before the door closed.

As I readied myself for bed, my mind swirled with thoughts of what the next day might hold. A tour of the castle was definitely first on my list. But my last thought, before falling asleep, was of the enigmatic Kieran Ramsey. Somehow, I told myself, before I left this place, I was going to figure out what made him tick.

Chapter Three

The Apparition

It began raining during the night, which was not at all uncommon in England, especially at that time of year. In fact, I considered myself lucky that it hadn't been raining when I arrived. I awoke once to the sound of rain beating against the window, then drifted back to sleep. I had a horrible dream about some sort of hairy black monster sitting on my chest, crushing me; and I awoke with a gasp to find a black cat crouched on the bed beside me, as though ready to jump on me. I reached a hand out to him, and he dove through an opening in the drapes surrounding my bed. I threw the drapes aside to see where he went, but he was already gone. To my surprise, I found the window open on one side. I got up and shut it, noticing a puddle of water on the floor where the rain had come in. *How odd,* I thought. I could have sworn the window was closed when I went to bed. Perhaps it hadn't been fastened tightly and had blown open. I dismissed it from my mind and went back to bed.

I don't know how much time had passed before I was awakened from my slumber again, this time by a faint noise that sounded like weeping. I opened the bed drapes again and looked toward the window. A cold, clammy draft wafted across the room to me, and at the same moment, I beheld a figure standing by the window. It appeared to be a young woman with long, wavy blonde hair, wearing a long, lace-trimmed white nightgown and holding a candle. She turned away from the window to fix me with her ghostly eyes and a hollow, faraway voice drifted from her.

"*Leave this place. There is much sorrow here.*" Then she vanished before my eyes.

I blinked, but when I opened my eyes, she did not reappear. My heart pounded, and I quickly closed the drapes around the bed and lay back down. *Relax, Selena,* I told myself. *There's no such thing as ghosts.*

When I awoke in the morning, the rain had slowed to a drizzle, so I decided to confine my explorations to the inside of the castle, at least until the rain let up. I had heard no signs of life around me, and it was still rather early, so I curled up in bed with my notebook and pen. I decided to keep a journal of the events of my trip, and I wanted to write about my first meeting with Kieran, since it struck me as a very strange event. I couldn't seem to stop replaying in my mind my first meeting with him the night before; my brain insisted on putting the whole exchange on "rewind" and then going through it all again. Kieran had given me a very strange feeling, the like of which I had never before experienced, and I couldn't figure out what it was. I kept thinking of his eyes, the uncanny way he looked at me. I wrote for about an hour and then washed up and got dressed, heading downstairs in search of breakfast.

I found the dining hall on my own and entered it to find the single place setting again. The servants must have been keeping an eye out for me, since the cook—Sissy, I believed her name was—brought out a massive breakfast of toast and jam, sausages, eggs, and fried tomatoes, with juice and a pot of tea. I had the feeling I was being watched and looked up to see the lifeless glass eyes of the mounted deer head above the fireplace eyeing me coldly. *What a disgusting trophy to put in a room where people eat,* I thought; though obviously I was the only one eating.

I finished my breakfast and still there was no appearance by my hosts. I wandered around, down some long, dark, and forbidding corridors, until I came upon a large room, which I later discovered was called the "Great Hall." It seemed to have an even loftier ceiling than the dining hall, and long, narrow windows lined the walls on either side of the room, facing east and west. Still more portraits, some of them quite massive, hung on the walls. At the south end of the room, an ornately carved permanent screen separated the entrance from the rest of the room, with a minstrels' gallery above and three smaller Gothic windows above that. On this screen wall hung racks of heavy, much-decorated swords, while at the opposite end of the room was a rack with thinner, more elegant-looking blades and fencing foils. There was very little in the way of furniture, just a couple of tables shoved against the wall and a few odd chairs that looked as though they had been dumped there for want of a better place to put them. Surely this hall must have been the scene of many balls in years past. I slowly walked around the perimeter of the room, studying each portrait in turn and wishing they at least had name plaques on them. One portrait in particular caught my eye. It was of a young knight in a suit of armor, holding his helmet under his arm as he gazed serenely from his spot on the wall. His other hand rested on the hilt of a large, heavy-looking sword. A plait of long, golden brown hair hung down over one shoulder, and he seemed to be looking right at me from pale blue eyes framed by slightly heavy lids. He had the same fair complexion and finely shaped eyebrows as Kieran and most of the other men in the family, judging from the portraits; but his lower lip was fuller than Kieran's, and the end of his nose was larger and more rounded. He also had a sweeter, more angelic facial expression; and as I looked at him, I was reminded of Saint George after slaying the dragon, or perhaps the Archangel Michael, standing nobly by the gates of heaven to defend it from Lucifer and his angels. It was rather pleasant to know that I had an ancestor who was so attractive, though it also left me wondering why couldn't *I* meet a guy like that—preferably one who wasn't related to me?

I looked up when I heard footsteps, to see Eugenia walking across the Great Hall to greet me. "Good morning, my dear," she said with a winsome smile. "I trust you had a good night's sleep?"

"Oh, yes. Thank you," I replied, choosing not to mention the ghostly woman, or the cat.

"And I trust breakfast was to your satisfaction?"

"Oh, yes. Thank you. Aunt Eugenia…" I hesitated, as suddenly I remembered that I had meant to ask Kieran why I had been left to dine alone and could not for the life of me figure out why I hadn't. I thought I'd broach the subject with someone more approachable. "Why do I always seem to eat by myself?"

"I get up so dreadfully early, and the lads stay up till all hours and then sleep so late they never eat breakfast. I see you've found the portrait gallery."

The abrupt way that Eugenia shifted gears seemed to indicate that she didn't want to pursue the topic of mealtimes any further, so I decided not to press the matter.

"Who is this?" I asked, indicating the young knight.

"Why, that's…another…Philip de Montfort. He fought in the Crusades. He died when he was 23."

"How tragic. Did he die over there, or at home?"

"I believe he took ill and passed away on the way home. Poor lad. He never married, either."

Eugenia seemed obsessed with marriage and children. I wondered whether perhaps she was getting older and wanting grandchildren.

"Have you drawn up a family tree?" I asked.

"Oh, indeed." Eugenia laughed. "It's quite large, and I've found it took up several large pieces of paper."

"I'd very much like to see it, if I may," I said. "Perhaps you could help me match some of the faces in these portraits to the names on the family tree?"

"Certainly, luv."

"This is all very exciting to me. I never dreamed I had a family like this. If I'd known when I was a kid that my ancestors lived in a castle, I'd probably have put on airs!"

"Have you met either of the lads yet?"

"'The lads'? Oh, you mean—yes, I made Kieran's acquaintance last night."

"I'm a wee bit concerned about him. I think he stays home entirely too much. He doesn't socialize enough. He's always been like that."

"Even when he was in school?"

"What?"

"You said he went to Oxford."

"Oh, yes. Well, I don't know what he did when he was at school." She seemed distracted.

"When do I get to meet Philip?"

"Why, I hope today. I can't imagine where he's been hiding since you've arrived. That's really quite rude of him to not come introduce himself to our guest. I'll have to have a word with him."

I suddenly wished I hadn't said anything; I didn't want anyone to get into any trouble on my account. "It's all right, really," I said quickly. "I'm sure he has a good excuse. And I'm sure I'll see plenty of him while I'm here."

"Well, I certainly hope so."

Derek appeared in one of the doorways and quickly and somberly made his way across the room. He quickly signed something to Eugenia, who nodded and said, "Thank you, Derek. I'll be ready in a few minutes." She turned to me. "I'm afraid I have an errand to run. I may be gone the rest of the day. Let Sissy or Ellen know if you need anything before Philip and Kieran get up."

"Okay," I said as Eugenia hurriedly followed Derek from the room. I continued my examination of the portraits in the Great Hall, till I came upon a door with a flower and leaf design carved into its panels. I pulled on the door, but it refused to give. I pulled harder, then tried pushing it inward by throwing my weight against it. It would not be moved in the slightest. I surmised that it must be locked, so I chose to leave the room through a different door. I wondered what lay on the other side of that door—perhaps it was something the family didn't want me to see. And of course that only made me all the more curious.

I stepped through a doorway and found myself in the inner ward, a sort of courtyard. It was drizzling out, so I chose to stay close under the overhang of roof that slanted out from part of the castle. I had seen the other side of it on the way in the day before, and I was beginning to figure out that it was this part of the castle that housed my bedroom, as well as the room where I had shared tea with Eugenia the day before, and the music room, where I had met Kieran. Its grey stone façade with its narrow windows and four towers, one on each corner, seemed to rise, tall and forbidding, into the gloomy sky. As I stood there, barely sheltered from the rain, I noticed the deathly quiet of the place and felt suddenly, creepily, very alone, until I spied a slight figure in jeans and a denim jacket, hunched over on the cobblestones beside the gatehouse. It appeared to be a young woman with short brown hair. I surmised it must have been the Ellen that Eugenia mentioned, since she was too slight of build and dark of hair to be Sissy, the cook. I wondered what she was doing on her hands and knees on the ground out in the rain, so I headed in her direction. As I got closer, I noticed she had a bucket and was dipping a scrub brush into it every few seconds and scrubbing the cobblestones. I stopped some distance away and wondered why someone would do such a job in the rain, when a whinny suddenly broke the silence and I quickly looked around for its source. My eye fell on a long, low building against the castle wall, and I hurried over to it. As I suspected, it was a stable, and as I entered it I smelled hay and leather and that animal smell one associates with stables. Three fine horses stood in the stalls. Being a city girl, I don't know very much about horses; I could tell only that one was black, one was white, and one was brown, and they were very beautiful animals, with glossy coats and luxuriant manes. I approached the brown one, who looked the friendliest.

"Hello, there," I said softly, hoping to win its trust. "What's your name?"

"I don't think she'll tell you," said a masculine voice from behind me. I spun around, my hand flying to my chest in surprise and near fright. A young man dressed in black, with a very antique-looking cobalt blue jacket left hanging open over his shirt, stood in the doorway. I could not really see his face very well at first, since it was overcast outside and rather dark inside the stable; but he soon stepped over to stand by the white horse, stroking its muzzle as he offered me a closer view of his profile. He had long, golden brown hair that fell in soft waves to the middle of his chest and a fair, flawless complexion. He slowly turned to look at me, and my mouth nearly fell open in surprise. His resemblance to the saintly-looking young knight whose portrait hung in the Great Hall was most astonishing.

"*You* must be Philip," I said, when I could find my voice.

A slow, but very charming, smile spread across his face. "Cousin," he said graciously, reaching for my hand.

"I think we're probably so distantly—"

Philip put up his other hand. "Not another word. You are family, and 'cousin' is how we think of you. Please feel welcome here." He kissed my hand, in a gesture that reminded me briefly of Kieran, but only briefly; Philip's manner seemed more forthright and honestly charming, with none of Kieran's elegant smirkiness. As he raised his eyes to look into mine, I thought I saw there a gentleness and strength of spirit that I found most becoming. I could get used to a guy like this, I thought.

"Please forgive me for not coming out to meet you sooner," he said smoothly, "but I wasn't feeling well."

"Oh, that's quite all right," I said. "I understand." At that moment, I think I would have forgiven Philip nearly anything.

"Do you ride?" he asked, stroking the white horse's muzzle again.

"Me? No. I mean, I've never learnt." I remembered what Eugenia said about Philip's being a good rider and that he might teach me. Perhaps he would let me start by riding with him, sitting in front of him with his arm around me. The thought made me tingle.

"I could teach you," he said.

"Okay," I said. "I'll give it a try."

Philip cast a glance outside. "We'll have to wait till this rain lets up. I wouldn't think you'd want to take your first lesson in a downpour."

I laughed, somewhat self-consciously. "No, I guess not."

"You can start out on Ianthe," Philip said, stroking the brown horse's nose. "She's very gentle."

"I suppose the white one is yours," I said. I looked down the row of stalls at the black horse. He was snorting and pacing in his stall, and perhaps it was my imagination, but I thought I detected a look of ferocity in his eye. "Let me guess—the black one is Kieran's."

"Very good," Philip said with obvious pleasure. "You can match a man with his mount? I take it you must have made my cousin's acquaintance already. My *other* cousin," he corrected himself.

"Yes, I rather stumbled upon him last night while he was playing his violin."

"He could best the devil himself, wouldn't you say?"

"He's very good. Has he ever played for anyone? For an audience, I mean?"

"Not to my knowledge. Kieran tends to keep to himself most of the time. So, what do you think of our fair England? And our noble castle?"

"Very impressive. The people over here are quite charming. Very different from what I'm used to."

"Americans are impolite?"

"Well, not always. Some are, but...well, that's not really what I meant. I don't know *what* I meant. Oh—"

Philip gave me a winsome smile. "If you're representative of Americans, I should think 'twould be nothing to complain about."

I figured this was a compliment, and flushed accordingly.

"Could I show you round?" Philip offered.

"Oh—sure. I was going to ask Eugenia about some more of those portraits, but she took off somewhere."

"My pleasure." Philip led me back to the Great Hall, and as we stepped into the room, I couldn't resist saying, "There's one portrait that looks an awful lot like you."

"Oh, you saw that one, did you? The other Philip de Montfort? Or should I say, *one* of the other Philip de Montforts? I believe there's been three or four. Yes, I've been told I'm his reincarnation. Isn't that absurd?"

I laughed. "Yeah."

Philip stopped in front of a painting of a dashing-looking man in a royal blue coat, with dark wavy hair and a steely gaze. "Now, there's one of your ancestors," Philip said. "Sir John Ramsey."

I studied the portrait more closely, feeling as though I were staring history in the face—literally. Old portraits seemed so much more fascinating when you discover that they're your own family.

"Seventeenth century?" I guessed, trying to judge by his clothing.

Philip appeared pleased. "Very good."

"What can you tell me about him?"

"I understand he was a bit of a rogue."

"If he's a Ramsey, he must be one of Kieran's ancestors too, right?" It didn't take a genius to figure that one out, especially considering Sir John's dark hair and hypnotic eyes. It was *obvious* he had to be one of Kieran's ancestors.

"Actually," Philip said thoughtfully, "I think *you're* the one descended from him. I believe Kieran goes back to Sir John's uncle. I suppose that makes you a closer relation to him than to me."

"Not by much," I laughed. "I do hope I get to see that family tree. This is all very fascinating, but I'm getting kind of confused."

"Why are you so intent on seeing the family tree?"

I was stunned for a moment. "Well...I thought that was why I was here. Eugenia went to all the trouble of tracking down all the living descendants, with the intention that we—in reality, I—would also benefit from her research. We all want to know where we come from, don't we? And like they say, 'Blood is thicker than water.'"

"Who says that?" Philip asked quickly.

"Why...people. It's an old saying. You don't have that saying over here?"

"I suppose I've heard it," Philip said, suddenly flippant. "I do believe it's stopped raining. Would you care to ride?"

"Well...okay. Sure." I puzzled over how he knew the rain had stopped, but as I followed him outside, I found that it was indeed true. The sky was, however, still grey and gloomy.

We walked to the stables and Philip called for Ellen. The young woman who had been scrubbing the cobblestones straightened up and hurried over. She was probably no more than eighteen or nineteen, with short brown hair and an extremely pale, almost pallid, complexion. She was shorter than I, and very thin, with prominent cheekbones and large, frightened-looking dark eyes. At least, that was the impression I got upon first seeing her face. She looked at Philip with those big, round eyes as though she were expecting terrible news.

"Saddle up Valiant and Ianthe," Philip told the young woman. "Miss D'Agostino and I are going for a ride."

Ellen bobbed her head and scurried away. "I've never heard of someone having a female stablehand," I remarked. "That's a refreshing change."

"Why is it a change?"

"I wouldn't want to think you people were *too* old-fashioned," I said with a smile.

"You find us old-fashioned?"

"In some ways, well…" I didn't want to offend Philip, but it seemed to me that living in a castle, kissing a woman's hand, and the rather stilted way that Kieran, Philip, and Eugenia talked—not to mention Kieran's and Philip's style of dress—qualified as being "old-fashioned."

"I didn't mean anything by it," I said quickly. "I meant it as a compliment. I wish there was more of it back home."

Philip's face relaxed into that glorious smile. "You must think of this as home…whilst you are here, of course."

Ellen brought the two horses, the reins of one in each hand.

"The first thing to be learnt, of course, is mounting," Philip said. "As I said, Ianthe is very gentle and accepting. She's taken a lot of riders. You must start by putting your foot in the stirrup and boosting yourself up. Here, let me help you."

Philip placed his hands upon my waist as he very nearly lifted me up into the air. I felt a current of excitement course through my body at his touch, at the same time marvelling at his strength. He wasn't very much bigger than I, but there was a lot of power in those arms, and my heart pounded as for one brief moment I thought of their holding me. Then the terror set in—I was sitting on a real, live horse, and I had *no* idea what I was doing.

"Very good," Philip said approvingly, nimbly mounting the white horse. "Now take the reins."

Philip was very patient with me, leading me slowly around the inner ward several times and not rushing the horse when he sensed I was nervous or uncomfortable. Ellen stood in the stable doorway, knitting her brow and chewing on her lower lip. I wondered whether she was concerned I might fall off, or if perhaps she was just another sour individual like Derek. But I didn't have much attention to spare the stablehand then; I was too busy just trying to stay on the horse.

When Philip was satisfied that I could stay on Ianthe without falling off, he led me through the gates into the countryside beyond at a leisurely canter. Not far from the castle walls, to the northeast, lay some woods. Philip headed directly for the trees, following a path that was slightly muddy from the rain. I looked up at the branches that crisscrossed over our heads, bursting with new green buds. All around us the earth seemed new and green and alive. I looked over at Philip sitting leisurely on Valiant, and once more could not help making the comparison between him and the young knight in the portrait who bore the same name. I could envision his wearing a suit of armor, sitting astride that proud white horse, leading his countrymen into battle.

"Peaceful here, is it not?" Philip observed.

"Yes," I agreed. "Very peaceful."

"This forest hasn't changed much for...many, many years. I think it's been here since the castle was built."

"Really?"

"Look how thick the trunks are on some of these trees. And the old maps show the woods here, about five hundred meters from the outer walls."

"If I had grown up here, I would have come out here a lot," I said. "Where I grew up, we had a treehouse in the backyard. I used to spend hours there. It was my special place to be alone." I smiled to myself at the memory. "I would pretend that was my castle in the clouds, that I ruled as far as the eye could see." Suddenly, my childhood fantasies seemed foolish and embarrassing. "I've always had an overactive imagination. I guess that's why I became a writer."

Philip was regarding me intently. "I would really like to read your books."

"Oh, I don't think they're anything that would interest you."

"Of course they would interest me. What are they about?"

"They're for teenagers. They're about teenagers and their different problems, like one about a boy whose parents get divorced and he doesn't get along with his new stepfather, one about a girl who falls in love with a guy who won't give her the time of day...that sort of thing."

"Why wouldn't that interest me? *You* interest me. Aren't your books like little pieces of yourself?"

"I...I suppose. I guess I never really thought of it that way."

"Let me ask you something. If you spent your childhood dreaming of castles, why did you choose to write about something so...ordinary?"

"I don't know. Maybe because my own adolescence was so unrewarding, so alone...I wrote about the things I never did, the people I never was. As I grew up, I kept writing about it because it was all I knew. I've never been like other people. I think more than I *do*."

"It's never too late...to start living the life you've always dreamed of."

No sooner had Philip spoken these words, than the thunder of hoofbeats sounded behind us. I turned to look, and saw a dark figure on horseback galloping down the path towards us. He stopped when he reached us, reining in his horse, despite the animal's obvious desire to keep going.

During the time of my childhood when I had chosen one Halloween to masquerade as an Aztec priestess, I had read every book I could get my hands on about the Aztec people and their culture. I remember being saddened by the accounts of how the Spanish conquistadors had nearly annihilated the Aztecs and destroyed their culture, and one scenario in particular remained vivid in my mind nearly twenty years later: how the Aztecs, upon first seeing the Spaniards' horses, were terrified, thinking that horse and rider were one beast. At the time I thought that rather strange—couldn't they see the man had legs?—but now, looking at Kieran, with his long black hair, dressed all in black and sitting regally astride a magnificent midnight-black stallion, I think I understood a little of the Aztecs' awe. The horse reared up on its hind legs, pawing the air with his forelegs and snorting, and I couldn't help but feel a profound admiration for Kieran, who retained control of the animal and seemed totally unphased by its antics. *I* would have found myself sitting on the ground.

"I didn't know you were going riding today," Kieran said.

"'Twas just a spur-of-the-moment thing, cousin," Philip replied smoothly. "I didn't think you'd be interested."

Kieran looked at me with his unreadable stare and asked, "I trust you slept well, dear cousin?"

"Well, the accommodations were quite comfortable…"

"But?" Kieran raised his eyebrows, looking ready to become offended.

"I slept fine, thank you." I thought better of mentioning the phantom woman, deciding not to let my "cousins"—since that was obviously what they wanted to be regarded—think I was some sort of hysterical female. Philip seemed satisfied with my reply, but I could tell from the look on Kieran's face that he wasn't fooled for a moment. I had a feeling I was going to have to watch myself around him.

Kieran took up a position on the other side of me as we led our horses deeper into the forest. "You probably find this place primitive," he said. "You're probably longing for your flushable toilets and your electrical lights."

"Oh, I'm sure I'll get used to it," I said. "It's probably good for me. Otherwise I might take those things for granted. By the way, whose cat was that in my room last night?"

Kieran and Philip exchanged a look across me. "Cat?" Philip said blankly.

"Yes, a cat. A black cat, to be exact."

"We haven't any cats," Kieran said.

"But there was this black cat in my bed, and it jumped out and just seemed to disappear."

"'Twas a dream, dear cousin," Kieran said.

"It was *not* a dream. Because I had just woken *up* from a dream, and there was this cat. And then I got up and shut the window, because the rain was coming in. And I don't remember leaving that open, either."

"Must have been a stray," Philip said.

"Where could it have come from?" I asked.

"Why, the village, of course." Philip didn't seem concerned in the least, as though he were used to finding strange cats in his own bed all the time. If they couldn't come up with a more plausible explanation for the cat, I certainly wasn't going to mention the woman in white.

"I'll race you to the old oak," Kieran said, taking off. Philip kicked his horse's flanks and galloped after him, leaving me alone on Ianthe.

"Hey, wait, you guys!" I shouted after them, not really wanting to be left alone my first day on a horse. The other two horses were racing hell for leather down the path, kicking up a fine spray of mud. Kieran obviously won, since I saw him wheel his horse around first. I reached them several minutes later, not daring to go any faster than a very slow walk.

"You only won because your horse is faster," Philip said.

Kieran smiled smugly. "You're such a sore loser, cousin. Still won't admit that I'm the better rider."

"Because you're not. Only a more foolhardy one." Philip started further down the path, and I followed him, not waiting for Kieran. But before I could catch up with Philip, Kieran drew abreast of me, turning to stare intently at me and lowering his voice as he said, "So, what *really* happened last night?"

"Nothing," I said, trying to keep my eyes straight ahead.

"You think I believe that?"

I turned to look at him then, and once I made the mistake of looking into his eyes, I felt unable to look away. Could those dark, unreadable eyes look right through me, into my soul?

"It was just a dream," I said.

"You mean there was something besides the cat?"

"It was *just* a *dream.* I had a bad *dream,* all right?"

Kieran nodded, but his eyes seemed to be saying, *Yeah, sure. Right.*

"What is keeping you two?" Philip demanded. I urged my horse forward, turning away from Kieran, but I could still feel his eyes on me. I willed myself to not look back at him, but my resolve wavered, and I stole a glance at him to see whether he was still staring at me. He was, with that infuriating little smirk of his, and I quickly turned back around.

When we came out of the woods, Kieran spurred his mount forward, leaving Philip and me behind. I watched as the black horse jumped a low wall and kept going.

"Don't pay him any mind," Philip said. "He loves to show off."

I watched Kieran and his horse grow smaller on the horizon as darker clouds began rolling across the sky. "I think it's going to rain again," I said.

"Yes, we'd best head back. Let Kieran get soaked if that's what he wants."

We made our way back through the forest. "So, you and Kieran and Aunt Eugenia are the only de Montforts left in England?" I asked.

"Yes. Just the three of us."

"Are both Kieran's parents dead?"

"Yes."

"He doesn't have any brothers and sisters?"

"He had a brother and two half-sisters, but yes, they're all dead. Everyone else is dead. No one in our family lives to a ripe old age. Kieran has maybe fifteen years left, I have perhaps twenty."

"That's a terrible thing to say!" I exclaimed. "You don't know when you're going to die—when *anyone's* going to die. Aunt Eugenia seems to be hanging in there."

"Eugenia's a rare case. She's one of the few family members who's lived to see her fiftieth birthday."

"My mother died when she was forty-four," I said quietly. "Nine years ago, when I was only nineteen. She had cancer."

"I'm very sorry, Selena."

"She had breast cancer. They're not sure how she got it. She never went in for mammograms or any kind of checkups since I was born and they didn't discover it until it was too late. I'm so scared sometimes. I don't want to die like that. My mother barely got to see me grow up. She never lived to see me get my books published. She never got a chance to be proud of me."

"I'm sure she had plenty of chances for that," Philip said gently.

I looked into Philip's eyes, comforted by the gentleness and compassion I saw there. I felt I could tell him anything. "I don't want to die," I said, in little more than a whisper. "It scares me to…well, death."

Philip reached for my hands with one of his, giving them a firm squeeze. "You're not going to die," he said. "You just said yourself that no one knows when they will go."

"It's hard for me to be positive and objective when I'm talking about myself. I went to a psychiatrist a couple of times after my mother died, because I was having trouble coping with her death. He said I had—I think he called it 'thanophobia'—'fear of death.'"

"Spring is in the air now, Selena. New life is beginning. You must put your fears aside now. It is time now for renewal, for enjoying life. I see I shall have to work especially hard to see to it that you enjoy your stay here."

A large raindrop splattered on my nose. "Uh-oh."

"We must hurry!"

"I can't ride fast, Philip!"

"Of course you can!"

"No, Philip, wait! I can't!"

"Get on with me. Ianthe knows the way back."

I climbed onto Valiant, sitting in front of Philip, who sent Ianthe on her way with a slap to her rear. Putting one arm around me, Philip took the reins in his other hand and we raced for the castle.

I scarcely noticed the rain that came down in a sudden downpour, drenching us; the intoxicating closeness of Philip's body was all my mind would allow itself to consider. I tried to remind myself that he was *family;* but a little voice in the back of my head—probably the same little voice that, when I was a child, liked to tell me my mother wouldn't notice if I took only *one* cookie—was telling me, "But he's so *distantly* related." It was only against the law to marry your *first* cousin, right? Philip and I had to be cousins about a hundred times removed. It was about the same as not being related at all—wasn't it?

But Philip probably didn't see it that way. His insistence that he be allowed to call me "cousin" because I was "family" put a real damper on things. He had apparently already defined our relationship in his own mind, and there was no room for romance in there. I knew it was hopeless.

When we got back to Cormoran, Ellen was waiting for us outside the stables. We dismounted and ran inside as the young stablehand brought Philip's horse back to its stall.

"Go to the parlor and remove your shoes," Philip instructed me. "I'll get Sissy to bring some towels."

I removed my shoes in the hallway and went upstairs to the parlor where I had shared tea with Eugenia the day before. My socks were so full of water, they made squishy noises as I moved. I was going to seek warmth at the fireplace, when I stopped in my tracks and gave a small, involuntary gasp.

I had not been expecting to see a slender male figure, clad only in a pair of black trousers, wringing out his long black hair in front of the fireplace. The drops splattered on the hearth, making the flames of the roaring fire sizzle. His clothes were spread out over a chair and his boots were drying in front of the fire. Straightening up and flipping his wet hair out of his face, Kieran turned and fixed me with his hypnotic eyes. Even barefoot and barechested, he surrendered none of his dignity as he eyed me and said, "You'd best remove those wet clothes before you catch your death of cold."

"Well, I certainly don't intend to do it *here,*" I said indignantly.

"A gentleman such as myself would never suggest such a thing," Kieran said glibly. "Or perhaps you are forgetting that you're a lady?"

I was seized by a terrible urge to hit him, one which I fought hard to resist. At that moment, Sissy entered, carrying a small stack of towels. Kieran took them from her and said, "Some more towels for the lady. And be quick about it." Sissy cast Kieran the briefest of annoyed looks before marching out the door. He handed me the top towel from the stack, which I snatched from his hand without a word. Kieran began slowly drying his hair with one of the other towels as he watched me dry myself, the vaguest hint of amusement playing about the corners of his mouth and eyes. I noticed for the first time that he had a thick, intricately carved silver ring in his left ear. I wondered why I hadn't seen it before. Perhaps his hair had been covering it.

"How did you get back already?" I asked, trying not to look at Kieran's smooth, bare chest and thin, sinewy arms.

"I'm very fast."

"You must be."

"Almost as fast as my horse." Kieran gave me a sly smile.

Sissy returned with more towels. I took a couple of them and said, "I'm going to my room to change. If Philip comes back, tell him I'll be right down."

"I'll tell him you tired of waiting for him," Kieran said with a wicked gleam in his eye.

"*No,* don't say that." I didn't want to admit that he was making me nervous. "Tell him I'll be down when I've dried off and changed."

"Of course, m'lady."

I frowned at him, certain that he was inwardly laughing at me again. I turned and stalked out of the room, as best I could with my squishy socks.

Upstairs in my chamber, I stripped off my wet clothes, spread them over some chairs, dried myself off, and rummaged through my suitcases for something else to wear. I eyed with disgust the hairdryer I had packed. I had figured that even *castles* nowadays had electricity. This was *England,* not some primitive Third World county. I recalled Kieran's sarcastic remark about "flushable toilets and electrical lights" as I furrowed my brow. Sure, *he* could laugh. He'd probably lived at Cormoran all his life; he was used to letting his hair air-dry and relieving himself in a cold stone hole. I decided that if I had to rough it while I was here, I would do so gracefully. I wasn't going to give anyone in this household any reason to consider me spoiled. Especially not Kieran.

Since I was supposed to be staying for a couple of weeks, I thought perhaps I would unpack and put my clothes into the large wardrobe next to the bed. After putting my clothes away and stowing the suitcases under the bed, I tried to untangle my hair with a wide-toothed comb and then went downstairs.

To my relief, Kieran was no longer in the parlor, although his clothes were. The strains of a violin coming from across the hallway left no doubt as to his whereabouts. Someone had left a full tea service on a small table near the fireplace, so I helped myself. Dark had fallen, and rain was beating against the windowpane. I sat by the fire, drinking tea and occasionally combing my fingers through my damp hair in an effort to speed its drying. After my second cup of tea, I was becoming concerned about what had happened to Philip; so, not really wanting to, but seeing no alternative, I forced myself to walk across the hallway to what I suppose would be called the music room.

"Kieran!" I said loudly. Kieran stopped mid-note, slowly opening his eyes and looking at me from their tops.

"Aye, m'lady?"

I tried to ignore his snide tone and asked, "Where's Philip?"

"Out," Kieran said simply.

"What?"

Kieran lowered his violin and eyed me with annoyance. "He's gone *out*."

"Out where? In this weather? And dark falling, besides? Where did he go? Why didn't he say he was going somewhere?"

"You're forgetting we Britons are quite used to the rain. And I was not aware Philip had to ask your permission to go somewhere." He placed his violin back on his shoulder, settling it under his chin.

"Wait just one minute! Don't you cut me off like that!" I demanded. Kieran's arm stopped in mid-air as he began to lift his bow, his eyebrows arching in apparent surprise. "What's with you people? You just take off all of a sudden with no explanation whatsoever, to just leave me dangling, never knowing what's going on!"

"You certainly have the Irish temper, don't you? That must come from your father's side."

"There is nothing wrong with my temper!"

"Perhaps you are also forgetting, dear cousin, that we also have lives of our own round here. We are not all your servants, waiting for your beck and call."

"I didn't say you were!"

"Philip was called away on business. He may not be back until late."

"And you knew this, but didn't bother to come tell me?"

Kieran gave me his coy smirk. "It seems you do not enjoy the pleasure of my company, m'lady."

His eyes were boring into me again, making me feel the heat of their intensity. "I never said that," I said in a small voice.

Kieran smirked again. "That is certainly the impression you give, m'lady. Perhaps 'tis a *false* impression?" He did not wait for me to reply, but went on. "Have a drink with me."

"All right," I said.

Kieran put down his violin and bow and walked over to the sideboard where he kept his wine. I looked at the back of his fresh white shirt, remembering seeing him shirtless in the parlor, how thin he was. I wondered if perhaps he drank all the time instead of eating. There had been a lot of alcoholism on my mother's side of the family, although she had been a teetotaller herself. Perhaps there was an alcoholism gene in the de Montfort family or, at least, one for self-destruction.

Kieran brought the two glasses of wine, but did not offer a toast; he simply clicked his glass against mine before raising it to his lips. I took a sip from my glass.

"What's wrong with this? It tastes kind of funny."

"'Tis nothing 'funny' about it. 'Tis an old family label."

I drank the rest of the wine in my glass, and Derek entered the room and signed to Kieran.

"Your supper is ready, m'lady," Kieran informed me.

"*My* supper? Aren't you eating?"

"No. Not tonight." He walked over to the sideboard and poured himself another glass of wine. "Please excuse my absence, my dear cousin." He raised his glass in a salute. "*Bon appetit.*"

I had a bad feeling in the pit of my stomach as I followed Derek to the dining hall. Somehow, I didn't feel hungry, either.

Chapter Four

The Dream

I ate dinner without enthusiasm, wondering on what "business" Philip could have been called away. Why hadn't he—or Kieran—said anything to me? I thought that was rather rude behavior on the part of such otherwise excruciatingly proper people. I tried to tell myself I was just being hypersensitive, but it didn't make me feel any better. I didn't like eating in that big, dark hall by myself, especially with that damned deer head eyeing me.

I wasn't sure what to make of Kieran. I remembered Eugenia's saying he stayed up late and then slept in, so I wondered whether perhaps he spent the night drinking and then had to sleep it off. He had to be an alcoholic, I reasoned—that must have been why I never saw him eating. And if he scarcely ate, that would explain why he was so thin. He definitely had less meat on him than either Philip or Eugenia, although they were both slender themselves. The thing that really puzzled me was that Kieran certainly never *acted* as though he were drunk or had a hangover. The first time I had seen him that day had been galloping down the forest path, a man in total control of both his actions and his wits. I had seen people with hangovers before, and they didn't act like Kieran.

After dinner, I thought to go to my room to write in my journal, as well as a letter to Valerie. I could already envision her reaction when I told her about Philip—"Oh, Sel, he sounds *gorgeous.* Imagine marrying some British gentleman-type and living in a castle! Damn!" (Protests from me.) "I mean it, Sel. Grab him and hang on with both hands!"

As I entered the gatehouse and headed up the stairs, I could hear a jingly tune coming from the music room. It wasn't a violin, and it wasn't a piano, but I wasn't certain just what it was. Overcome by curiosity, I poked my head through the doorway. Kieran sat playing an upright instrument that vaguely resembled a piano. A large black dog crouched on the floor near him. Despite the fact that I had made no sound, Kieran slowly turned his head and stared at me.

"Has Philip come back?" I asked. Kieran slowly shook his head, never missing a note. The dog started to get up, baring his teeth and snarling.

"Mephistopheles!" Kieran said sharply, and the dog backed down. He stopped playing and turned to face me. "I'm afraid he's not very friendly."

I wondered anew about the black cat, thinking that no feline in its right mind would want to visit a household with a dog like this.

"He usually stays out in the stables, guarding the horses," Kieran explained, as though he knew I'd been wondering why I hadn't seen the dog before.

"What are you playing?" I asked.

"I'm afraid I don't remember the name of it. 'Tis a very old tune, dating to about the early Renaissance."

"No, I meant the instrument."

"A harpsichord. Have you never seen one before?"

"No, I can't say that I have, although I've heard of it."

"You don't see these very much anymore. This one has been in the family for over four hundred years."

"And it's still in a condition to be played?"

"We've taken good care of it. Actually, it has rather fallen out of favor. If it weren't for me, it would be just gathering dust."

"Who taught you to play?"

"My mother." Kieran gestured to a chair near the harpsichord. "Won't you have a seat, m'lady?"

I sat down in the proffered chair. "My mother influenced my musical tastes, too, I suppose," I said. "She turned me on to classical music when I was very small."

"You were close to your mother?"

When Philip asked me questions, he seemed interested and sympathetic. Somehow, Kieran seemed rather prying. Perhaps it was his eyes, the intent way he stared at me.

"Somewhat," I said carefully. "I never told her *everything*. But I was an only child, so I guess I was closer to my mother than a lot of people." I decided to turn the tables on him—asking *him* the questions for once. "What about *you?* Were you close to *your* mother?"

Kieran's eyes narrowed, as though he didn't like being questioned. "My mother always looked out for me…she pushed so that I would get things…she was adamant that I get the best possible education. She always wanted the best for me; she never settled for anything less."

"You didn't really answer my question," I said. "I asked if you were close."

"My mother was a very courageous person. She took on all the de Montforts single-handedly. Of course I loved my mother. But she never understood me."

I wondered to myself whether *anyone* could understand Kieran. He and Philip were so different, it was hard to imagine that they were related. But then, I couldn't get used to the fact that I was related to both of them.

"So, who is your favorite?" Kieran asked.

I blinked. "What?"

"Your favorite composer?"

"Oh," I said, relieved. "Bach, I suppose…or perhaps Beethoven …although I'm also very fond of Tchaikovsky."

Kieran nodded, and the look in his eyes seemed to tell me he was filing this information away in his brain for whatever reason. He slowly and carefully fingered a few keys.

"When I was in about the fourth grade, I wanted to take violin lessons, but my parents wouldn't let me," I said softly. "They insisted on making me learn the piano, which is okay, I guess, but I always yearned to learn the violin."

"Perhaps we have more in common than you think."

I wasn't certain what he meant by that, and I was afraid to ponder it. "I should go upstairs," I said quickly. "I want to write a letter to my best friend before I go to bed."

"You retire quite early, don't you?"

"I probably have jet lag. Tell Philip I'll see him tomorrow—if you see him before I do." I got to my feet.

"Shall I escort you to your room, dear cousin?" Kieran asked as he rose from his bench.

"No, thank you. I think I can find my own way this time."

"As you wish, m'lady." Kieran inclined his head. "I hope you have more *pleasant* dreams tonight."

***

I had promised Valerie a postcard, but since I hadn't been to town yet, and I didn't want anyone else reading what I had to say, I sat down and wrote her a letter.

Dear Val,

I made it to Castle Cormoran in one piece, and my bags made it all the way with me! I know I promised you a postcard, but I haven't been to town yet. Rest assured I will send one.

England seems quite charming—what I've seen of it. I hope to get out and explore more tomorrow. My relatives—I still have trouble getting used to that—are something else. I feel like I stepped back in time—there's no electricity or running water here, and their "toilet" is a hole in a slab of stone with a long, dark shaft that goes down to God knows where. Answering nature's call first thing in the morning is like parking your naked butt on an iceberg! (I can hear you laughing, Val.) Aunt Eugenia seems very sweet, but she's so terribly proper. Her son Philip is to die for. There's a painting in the castle here of a knight from the Middle Ages who looks just like him, and even has the same name. Isn't that weird? He's the perfect British gentleman—so cultured and polite, and he has the greatest British accent. He's teaching me to ride a horse! Can you believe that? I can't even ride a bicycle!

And I cannot forget to tell you about Philip's cousin Kieran. You really should meet this guy, Val, because I swear you've never met anyone like him. I don't even know how to describe him, except that the words "snide" and "enigmatic" come to mind. I have to be really careful what I say to him—he just gives me this really weird feeling.

Well, I'd better go. Tomorrow I'm going to take some pictures. Give Rufus a big hug and kiss for me and tell him I miss him. Take it easy, and I'll tell you everything in a couple of weeks!

Love ya!

Sel

P. S. Tell my dad you heard from me and everything's fine. He worries too much.

***

I fell asleep to the sound of rain beating against my window, coming down in great sheets. I thought to myself that if April showers truly brought May flowers, this place should really be blooming in about a month.

As I slept, I dreamed about the rain, coming down on me as I hurried inside. I walked into the parlor as I had that day, to find Kieran drying himself by the fire. He slowly looked over at me, giving me a look that seemed to bore straight through me, into my soul. "Where's Philip?" I asked.

Kieran put down his towel and slowly walked over to stand directly in front of me. He bent his head so that his lips were only a couple of inches from mine, and I couldn't keep from staring at them. "Philip isn't here," he said in a hoarse whisper. "He'll never know." It seemed an agonizingly long moment before his lips finally reached mine, and it didn't even occur to me to struggle or push him away. I felt as though I were spinning wildly out of control, till suddenly I awakened with a start.

For a moment, I was completely disoriented. I looked at the dark green draperies surrounding the bed, and then I remembered. It was only a moment more before my dream came flooding back to me, and my face flamed. In my distrust of Kieran, I had never, up to that time, stopped to consider whether or not I found him attractive, so that my dream both surprised and embarrassed me. How could I dream about Kieran when there was Philip? I firmly told myself that it was just a silly dream and that I was going to forget about it; but, try as I might, I kept seeing his face, I kept hearing his voice. They seemed to mock me, so that I felt I would surely go mad. I hid my head under my pillow and tried in vain to will the memory of my dream to go away. But the more I tried, the more I seemed to hear his voice saying, "I hope you have more *pleasant* dreams tonight."

When I awoke again in the morning, it was fairly early, but I decided to get up and get my day started. The rain had stopped, but the sky was still overcast. I wondered to myself whether I would see the sun at all during my stay. I addressed my letter to Valerie and took it downstairs with me, intending to post it if I could get Derek to drive me into town.

I thought to explore the upstairs of the gatehouse, where my room was located, but found only closed doors. I didn't want to open any of them, because I figured they were bedrooms. A rhythmic snoring came from behind one of the doors, confirming my suspicion. I surmised that it must be either Kieran or Philip—the possibility that it could be Eugenia never occurred to me, since I couldn't imagine such a great noise coming from such a proper lady.

I took my breakfast in the dining hall, alone again, and afterwards wandered the grounds, my letter to Valerie jammed in the back pocket of my trousers. I didn't know where to find Derek, but I knew he had to be prowling about somewhere. As I passed the stables, I saw Ellen sweeping some dirt out the doorway.

"Ellen?" I asked, trotting over to the doorway before she had a chance to disappear. Ellen looked up at me, with that same frightened and dismayed look I had seen on her face the day before. "Do you know where I might find Derek?" I asked.

Ellen shook her head, then made signs with her hands before taking up her broom again and going back to work. My heart sank. Not *another* mute servant! Oh, why had I never learnt sign language? *Because you never thought you'd be visiting your relatives in a castle who hire only mute people for servants, dummy,* I told myself.

I was just walking away from the stables, frustrated, when I spied Derek emerging from the doorway that led inside to the Great Hall. "Derek!" I shouted, flagging him down. Derek stopped in his tracks and gave me his usual sour face. I must say, I was not very impressed with the dispositions of the servants in this place. Somehow, I got the feeling that they all resented me.

"Could you give me a ride into town?" I asked, determined not to let his glum countenance daunt me. "I have a letter I'd like to mail, and I thought I'd get out and look around."

Derek shook his head no.

"What do you mean, no? Why not?"

Derek made a scribbling gesture on his left palm with his right hand.

"I don't have any paper with me," I said. "Upstairs in my room—"

Derek gestured for me to follow him, so I trailed him to the gatehouse. Once inside, he headed straight for the music room, to the sideboard where Kieran kept his wine, and began rummaging through its drawers until he found a pad of paper and a fountain pen. I thought to myself that I hadn't seen one of those in years. Derek scribbled a hasty note and handed it to me.

You're not to leave the grounds.

"Why not?" I demanded.

Derek scribbled on another sheet.

That's my orders.

"And who gave you these orders?" I asked, trying to hold my temper in check.

Master Kieran.

My temper flared then. How dare he! He had no right to keep me a prisoner there! "I demand an explanation," I said, "and I want it from him directly. Now—if I have to wake him myself!" I started out the door, but Derek jumped in front of me, barring my way. His eyes widened and his mouth opened in an expression that could only be described as one of horror, as he violently shook his head back and forth. I wondered whether perhaps Kieran slept in the nude, and Derek was mortified at the thought of my discovering his master in such a state.

"All right," I said, relenting. "I'll wait till he gets up to have a word with him. In the meantime, could you please mail this for me?" I handed Derek the letter. He nodded as he took it from my hand, then disappeared.

I turned around, and it was then that I noticed another door at the far end of the room. I was about to check and see where it led, when I remembered my camera, upstairs in my bedroom. I quickly went upstairs to get it, since I wanted to take advantage of the current lack of rain to take some photos of the castle and its grounds. I shot up a 36-exposure roll of film, and I was in the Great Hall when my film ran out, taking photographs of some of the portraits. As I rewound the film and removed it from my camera, Eugenia appeared.

"Good morning, Selena, my dear," she said warmly, the little crinkles deepening around her eyes. "Did you sleep well?"

"Yes, thank you," I said, already growing a little weary of the question.

"I brought the family tree," Eugenia said, "since you so wanted to see it." She produced a large, rolled-up piece of paper.

"Oh, terrific. Can we look at it here? Maybe you can identify some of these people for me." I gestured to the pictures on the walls.

"Certainly, luv." Eugenia led me to one end of the room, to a couple of small side chairs. I noticed once again the case containing several of the long, thin swords used for fencing.

"Does anybody use these any more?" I asked.

Eugenia sat down and put on a pair of reading glasses before looking up, seemingly distracted. "I say, what? Oh, those. Indeed. The lads make use of them. They're only fencing foils, you know. The real swords are over there." She flung a hand towards the opposite end of the hall. "Most of those are quite old. The one that Philip de Montfort—the Philip de Montfort who fought in the Crusades, of course—has in that portrait is there, as well as one dating back to the days of William the Conqueror."

"Which one belonged to the other Philip de Montfort?" I asked as I walked over to the other rack.

Eugenia got up and followed me. "This one, I think," she said, touching the hilt of a very heavy-looking broadsword. "Or was it perhaps this one? Come, let's look at the family tree." She walked back to her chair.

I stood looking at the swords. William the Conqueror—that had to be nearly a thousand years old! I couldn't even begin to imagine how much something like that must be worth, and to think of having it just sitting around in your house! Just about everything in this place—with the obvious exceptions, such as a CD player I had spied on the sideboard in the music room—had to be priceless antiques. The three horses in the stable were obviously of very high quality, and the family members all dressed very well, if somewhat old fashioned. I figured they must be loaded.

I sat down beside Eugenia as she unrolled the family tree. "I've been able to trace the family back to James de Montfort, who built this castle."

"When was that?" I asked.

"Work was begun on this castle in 1283. It was not completed until about 40 years later."

"Wow," I said, "that's a long time."

"Well, I suppose they had to stop and fight various wars and so forth. Perhaps at times it became a bit of a strain on their finances, as well."

Eugenia proceeded to tell me about nearly every person on the chart, so that after listening to her for what seemed like hours about all the Johns, Philips, Charleses, and Georges, my head began to spin. Finally, I noticed that the family tree went up to about the fifteenth century and stopped.

"Where's the rest of it?" I asked.

"Oh, it's on another sheet. I told you it was very large. We can discuss the rest of it at another time. Derek probably has tea waiting for us in the parlor." Eugenia rolled up the sheet of paper and removed her glasses. At the mention of Derek's name, I thought of asking Eugenia why I wasn't allowed to leave the grounds, but decided against it. Derek had said those were Kieran's orders, so I would take it up with him personally. I didn't want to get on Eugenia's bad side, if indeed she had one.

We had tea with scones—something I'd heard of but never before tasted—in the parlor. Eugenia regaled me with more tales of my ancestors' exploits, before saying she didn't feel well and was going upstairs to lie down. She left the family tree on the end table by the tea service, so I reached for it, unrolling it and poring over it again.

"That doesn't really tell you anything," a voice behind me said. I jumped and turned around, my heart feeling as though it had leapt up into my mouth. Kieran gave me a sardonic smile, obviously enjoying the fright he'd just given me.

"Do you have to sneak up on me like that?" I demanded, as he walked over to the fireplace, casually leaning against the mantel and facing me. "You nearly gave me a heart attack."

"You frighten easily, m'lady," Kieran said with a nasty gleam in his eye. "Are you afraid of the dark, as well?"

"No, I am not afraid of the dark."

"That's good. I wouldn't want you to be *uncomfortable*...have trouble *sleeping*." He was looking at me as though he *knew*...but of course I knew that was impossible. He couldn't read my mind, and he couldn't know about my embarrassing dream. But my face flamed just the same, and it must have been noticeably red, because Kieran then asked, "Did I say something to offend you, dear cousin?"

"No," I said, struggling to maintain my composure. "But I would like to know why you told Derek I can't leave the castle grounds."

Kieran idly picked up a poker and stabbed at the burning firewood with it. "'Tis for your own protection, m'lady."

"Protection from whom?"

"I don't mean to alarm you, cousin, but we have rather a lot of wolves round here."

"Wolves?"

"Yes. Which is why our stables are now located inside the inner ward. We can't be too careful."

"How are wolves going to be a threat to me if I'm riding with Derek in the car?"

"Selena," Kieran said, with what appeared to be patient irritation, "please believe me when I say that I have only your best interests at heart. 'Tis my duty to protect you whilst you are here. If anything happened to you, how could I answer to your father? So I must ask you not to leave the castle grounds unless you are in the company of either Philip or myself."

"But you always get up so damned late! How am I supposed to go anywhere?"

"I thought your visit was supposed to be here, with us."

"Of course, but I don't want to be cooped up. I want to be able to get out and see things."

"There's nothing here to see."

I was growing frustrated. "You can't keep me a prisoner here!"

"A prisoner?" Kieran looked offended. "Is that really how you view your stay here? As a prison sentence?"

"I'm about to," I snapped, and immediately regretted it when I saw the way Kieran's eyes narrowed and his mouth hardened into a thin, tight line. The effect was positively scary.

"I don't know what it is you're afraid of, dear cousin," Kieran said slowly, "but it needn't be I."

At that moment, much to my relief, Philip stepped into the room. "Selena," he said, nodding to me. He walked over to me and took both my hands in his and raised them to his lips. "I trust you're feeling well?"

I thought I saw Kieran scowling at the back of Philip's head before turning and becoming seemingly engrossed in jabbing at the logs in the fireplace again with the poker.

"I'm quite well, thank you," I said, and noticed that their somewhat stilted speech was starting to rub off on me.

"My cousin is not harassing you overmuch, is he?" Philip asked, casting a quick glance over at Kieran and trying to suppress a smile.

"Oh, no," I said flippantly, not wanting Kieran to know how much he disturbed me, "not anything I couldn't handle."

Kieran slowly looked over at me, a dark storm brewing in his eyes. They seemed to be saying, *You haven't seen anything yet.*

"What would you like to do this evening?" Philip asked graciously. "I'll accommodate you any way I can."

"I *would* like to get out and see the countryside," I said, "but it'll be dark soon."

"We can go for a ride," Philip said. "In the motor car, that is. I find it quite enjoyable to tool about after dark."

"Okay," I said. "Let me get a jacket."

"You needn't bother running all the way upstairs," Philip said. "I believe there's one in the music room. I'll get it for you."

"Thank you," I said as Philip strode from the room. I looked over at Kieran, who gave me a long look and then walked away. I wondered what that was for.

"Here you are," Philip said, returning with a green velvet jacket that he placed around my shoulders.

"This is beautiful," I said, examining it.

Philip smiled and ushered me from the room. "Don't be staying out too late," Kieran said loudly and sarcastically from the far side of the room as we left.

Philip called for Derek, who appeared seemingly from nowhere. "Fetch the motor car, Derek," Philip told him. "Miss D'Agostino and I would like a ride."

I felt a stab of disappointment as Derek nodded and scurried away. I had hoped to make the ride with Philip alone—although Derek was mute, he obviously was not deaf.

I got into the back seat of the old black Daimler with Philip, who sat very close to me. "Don't let Kieran bother you," he said confidentially.

"He can be rather intimidating, I suppose, but his bark is worse than his bite." He laughed as though this were very clever.

"How closely related are we?" I asked.

"Not very," Philip said, suddenly very serious.

"I don't look like anyone else in the family, do I? I guess my de Montfort genes—or Ramsey, or whatever—are pretty watered down, huh?"

"I don't know that I would put it that way," Philip said. "We're just more English than you."

"May I say something incredibly stupid?" I asked in a tiny voice.

"You may say whatever you wish."

"I love your accent. Where I'm from, people talk so flat and uninteresting. Like me."

"There is nothing either flat or uninteresting about you," Philip said in little more than a whisper, as he bent down to kiss me. I wasn't expecting it and instinctively pulled away.

"I forget myself," Philip said apologetically. "A gentleman should never force himself on a lady."

"You weren't forcing," I said. "You took me by surprise."

"You wouldn't report my lapse of manners to anyone else, would you?" he said in my ear, very softly, as he began to slowly kiss my neck.

"I wouldn't dream of it," I said, closing my eyes. When his lips found mine again, I allowed myself to return the kiss this time. But something made me feel guilty, and I pulled away again. "The rain is coming down really hard now," I said feebly.

"Yes, you're quite right. Derek, take us back."

I wasn't sure what was holding me back. Certainly I had been admiring Philip since we had met—he was unquestionably handsome, and he was easy to talk to, gentle of manner and a good listener. And surely he was right that we were really not closely related. We would have to go back a few hundred years to find a common ancestor. We were both unattached. So what was my problem?

"Are you all right?" Philip asked solicitously.

"I'm fine, thank you," I said. "I was just thinking about my mother." That really wasn't true, but I didn't know what else to say.

A look of gentle concern crossed Philip's face. "What about her?"

"Just that ...never mind."

"Please tell me."

Derek pulled up in front of the gatehouse then, and I was spared having to say anything further. Philip opened the door for me, and we ran inside to get out of the rain that was now coming down in great sheets.

There was no sign of anyone about when we dashed inside. For this I was grateful, since I didn't think I was up to dealing with Kieran at the moment. Philip must have seen my eyelids drooping, because he suggested I go to bed.

"I really would like a bath," I said.

"I'll have Sissy draw it for you. You do know where it is, don't you?"

"Yes, it's around the corner."

"Very good. I shall see you tomorrow, then. Goodnight, Selena."

"Goodnight, Philip," I said, just before he kissed me. I watched him stride down the hall, wishing I was going to be in England for more than a couple of weeks.

***

After soaking in the tub until my toes wrinkled, I stumbled down the hall to my room and fell into bed. I had fallen into a deep sleep, I know not for how long, when I was awakened by a scream. I snapped awake, every muscle tense, then told myself it was just one of the peacocks. I was just about to settle down, when I heard a faraway howl. It's just that big black dog, I told myself. But then I heard another howl, and another. There was more than one animal out there, making that noise. I suddenly remembered Kieran's warning about wolves, and, despite the gnawing fear in the pit of my stomach, I got out of bed, wrapping a blanket around myself, and stole over to the window.

A full moon shone on the inner ward below, giving everything a soft, shadowy glow. The rain had slowed to a fine drizzle, and standing by the old stone wall, with the bracing early spring air pushing its way through the open window, I felt chilly and damp down to the bone. I reached out to close the window, wondering why it was repeatedly being left open, when I thought I detected a blue mist hovering over the ground of the inner ward. I blinked, thinking at first that I must be seeing things; but when I looked again, it was still there, and it began to move, drifting over the cobblestones. It had no definite form or shape but, rather, kept shifting and changing as it headed toward the Great Hall, opposite the gatehouse. The only thing I could think of was that it was a ghost, and I screamed involuntarily. I ran from the room, yanking the door open and fleeing into the hallway, where I ran into something and screamed again.

A pair of strong hands grasped my upper arms, and I opened my mouth to scream a third time, when a low voice said, "Shhh," and I looked up and saw that it was only Kieran.

I pulled away from him, and his arms fell to his sides. He was barefoot, his shirt was open, and his hair mussed, looking as though he had just gotten out of bed. His eyes, however, didn't look sleepy in the least.

"There's something outside my window," I said, fighting to keep the hysteria from my voice.

"What is it?" Kieran looked skeptical.

"It might be a...a...a ghost or something. I don't know. It was this...it was like a...a blue mist or something."

"A ghost?" Kieran's look of skepticism deepened. "Blue mist?"

"Come see for yourself," I challenged him.

Kieran followed me into the room and I pointed out the window, across the inner ward. A bank of clouds was drifting by overhead, hiding the moon, but there was no sign of the blue apparition.

"I don't see anything now," Kieran said.

"It was just there," I insisted. "Heading in the direction of the Great Hall. And I heard wolves howling, too."

"Dear cousin," Kieran said with wearied patience, "even wolves have sense enough to get out of the rain."

"You don't believe me."

"I think perhaps your writer's imagination has run away with you."

"It was not my imagination. I can at least separate fantasy from reality."

"Indeed?" Kieran cocked an eyebrow. "Like the black cat in your bed?"

"I know what I saw."

"Perhaps you'd rather sleep in my room tonight?" Kieran suggested as he shut the window.

"With you?" My heart raced wildly at the thought of lying beside him in his bed, feeling his breath against my neck, his lips…I quickly clamped a firm lid on my emotions and said primly, "I'd rather not!"

Kieran looked at me as though I were a simpleton. "I meant that I would sleep in yours."

I drew myself up to my full height. I hoped my face didn't look as red as it felt. I was not going to present him with the image of an hysterical female. "I'll be fine right here."

"As you wish, m'lady." Kieran headed for the door. "If you need me, I am straight across the corridor."

"I would rather call on Philip," I said loftily.

"Very well, m'lady. Just remember who answered your scream." With that, he was gone.

Chapter Five

The Melody

I was still fuming at Kieran as I went back to bed. What made him think that I didn't know what I was talking about, that he always knew better than I did? Did he affect that superior manner because I was a woman, or because I was an American, or did he just act that way with everybody?

I was beginning to wonder whether I would ever get a good night's sleep in this place, as I lay in the position in which I felt most comfortable, curled up in the fetal position on my right side. I always lie that way when I first climb into bed. I was suddenly aware of a gentle movement behind me, as of someone else getting into the bed; but my senses were only hazy as I got drowsier, so I really didn't pay very much attention at first. I became aware of another body settling down beside me, fitting its contours into my own: a chest pressed against my back, another pair of knees and thighs behind mine. A hand slithered up under my nightgown, gliding up my left thigh and over my hip. A shiver ran through me and my heart began to beat faster. A low purr rumbled from the chest behind me. A hand brushed my hair off my neck and gently pushed my nightgown away from the same area, exposing more of my shoulder. The hand on my hip slowly rubbed up and down my thigh, and after making several passes, made the trip up my thigh on the inside of my leg. At the same time, a pair of sensual lips descended upon the curve of my neck and shoulder, travelling up my neck to the area behind my ear, as though they meant to devour me.

I involuntarily gasped at the delicious shiver that ran through me. "Oh, Philip," I whispered, reaching my left hand back to touch his hair.

"Philip be damned," a husky voice rasped in my ear, as the hand between my legs snaked up my torso and cupped itself over my breast.

"Kieran!" I shrieked, jerking away and flipping over, expecting to see his dark eyes mocking me, that self-satisfied smirk on his face. But the bed was empty.

I sat up, my chest heaving, and put a hand over my mouth, as if to force the word back inside. The last thing I needed was to have Kieran—and the rest of the household—hear me screaming out his name in the middle of the night. It was only a dream, I told myself. It doesn't even mean anything.

But I failed to find an explanation for myself for why it felt so real.

***

Eugenia was up early the next morning, and for the first time since my arrival, took breakfast with me. As she chattered away about more adventures of the de Montfort family, I tried, rather unsuccessfully, to listen; but my mind insisted on torturing itself over the night before. Something strange was going on here, I felt. For the first time, I realized how funny it seemed that Philip had made such a to-do about my being "family" and calling me "cousin," and then last night in the car he had suddenly been all over me. And what about that blue mist? Could it have been another manifestation of the ghost lady? I couldn't figure out what the blue mist could have been, if it wasn't a ghost—and the thought of staying at a haunted castle really gave me the creeps—and either Kieran didn't know about it, or he didn't want to admit he knew about it. And then Kieran himself bothered me immensely. I had run into him the moment I got out of the room, as though he had been waiting outside my door. But the worst thing was that which I was uncertain as to whether it was a dream or not. It still remained vivid in my mind, much more vivid than my dreams usually do; and when I am dreaming, my sense of touch and feeling is not nearly so sharp. I had a horrible feeling that Kieran actually had been there, that he had crept back in shortly after having come in and closed my window, probably with the intention of taking advantage of me while I was asleep. My outrage that he would stoop to such a low was overshadowed only by my humiliation of having responded to it. I had felt sure it was Philip only because my mind would not accept that it might be Kieran. How could I ever face him again?

After breakfast, Eugenia took me up to her room to look at some old photo albums. Looking at anything having to do with the family was an affair lasting for hours—she had to stop at every picture and explain everything. I wondered idly how she knew so much, and was about to ask her if she had any newer albums—with pictures taken since Philip and Kieran were born—when she suddenly straightened up and said she had some business to attend to and asked to be excused. As I walked down the corridor to my room, with the intention of getting my jacket, I stopped in front of my door and slowly turned around, looking suspiciously at the door that was almost straight across the hall from mine. "If you need me, I am straight across the corridor," I could hear Kieran's voice saying. Then I remembered something else he had said, on the night I had first met him: "I was only anticipating what you were going to say." So, he thought he knew me so well already, did he? Did he actually think he could read my mind? Had he, in his conceited self-assurance, known that I would respond to his touch? But only because I thought he was someone else, I quickly told myself. Perhaps a little too quickly.

I put on my jacket and went outside to the inner ward. I was just standing there, breathing in the brisk fresh air, when a voice behind me made me jump.

"Ready for another riding lesson?" Philip asked.

"Oh—Philip," I said, relieved.

"I didn't mean to frighten you," he apologized. "Did you sleep well?"

"Oh—yes. Thank you."

"I thought I heard a scream, but when I got to your room, Kieran was just coming out and said it was nothing."

My face flamed at the mention of Kieran's name; I hoped Philip didn't notice. "Oh—I just thought I saw something outside, but it must have just been my mind playing tricks on me. It does that sometimes when I'm overly tired."

"I kept you out too late," Philip said, looking repentant.

"Oh, that's quite all right," I said quickly. "I had a wonderful time."

Philip's face brightened. "I wouldn't want you to leave here with a bad impression…or not having enjoyed yourself."

"Oh, no worry," I said.

"Where shall we ride today?" Philip asked as we slowly headed for the stables.

"Oh…I don't know. Anywhere." I smiled sadly. "I think I have saddle sores from the last time."

Philip laughed. "Oh, you'll get used to it. In no time a'tall 'twill seem as though you've done it all your life."

I couldn't really envision that happening, but I smiled at him anyway. Philip helped me mount Ianthe, and we rode outside the castle grounds, away from the woods. I was on edge, always expecting to hear the approaching hoofbeats of Diogenes, Kieran's fearsome black stallion; but to my great relief—or perhaps, disappointment?—Kieran did not seem inclined to ride with us that day.

"What are you looking for?" Philip asked, catching a fervent glance I cast over my shoulder.

"Oh, nothing."

"You look as though you're afraid someone's following you."

"It's just...well, maybe I'm paranoid, but I'm starting to feel like Kieran is always creeping up on me."

Philip laughed. "Oh, don't pay him any mind." He quickly sobered. "Were you expecting him today?"

"Me? Oh, no."

"If you would rather his company than mine—"

"Oh, no, Philip! That's not it at all! I really enjoy being with you. I do."

Philip smiled again. My answer seemed to satisfy him. Although he was never anything less than extremely polite, I had the feeling that there was a very intense rivalry brewing between Philip and Kieran, and I hoped it didn't have anything to do with me. I remembered only too well Kieran's dark scowls and sarcastic remarks of the night before, when Philip had walked in on us in the parlor, and his suggestion that I enlist his aid when things frightened me in the night.

When we returned to the castle, Philip brought the horses back to the stables as I waited by the outside door of the gatehouse. A tidal wave of embarrassment swept over me as I saw Kieran emerging from the Great Hall and heading in my direction. I froze, knowing that he had already seen me and that there was no escaping him, and my face flamed as I remembered the previous night.

"Seen any more blue ghosts, m'lady?" Kieran said, with a trace of amusement, as he stopped a couple of feet in front of me.

"No, I have not," I said, standing tall and struggling to maintain my composure. I decided not to say anything about the other incident. If it really was a dream, I wasn't going to give Kieran the satisfaction of knowing about it. "You must have scared it off," I deadpanned.

"Any more black cats in your bed...m'lady?" he asked, his voice very low and a wicked gleam in his eye. I felt my face grow hot. He knew. Which meant—he had actually been there. I stood there and wished a hole would open beneath my feet and swallow me up.

"Stay out of my room," I sputtered. "And stay out of my bed. Don't get any more funny ideas, just because—"

Kieran smiled indulgently. "My *dear* cousin—I haven't had the *pleasure* of being *in* your bed."

I noticed particularly the emphasis he placed on the word "pleasure," and I found myself focusing on his lips as he said the word. I thought of the lips on my neck the night before being Kieran's lips, and my mind's eye gave me an intensely sharp image of his mouth against my flesh, causing my heart to jump up and pound painfully. My sense of mortification grew to such monstrous proportions, for a moment I thought it quite possible to die of shame. "You—" But nothing else would come out.

Kieran was obviously cherishing my discomfort. "My, but you certainly have an overactive imagination, m'lady. Or perhaps 'twas another of your rather—vivid, shall we say?—dreams. Do you know what they say about dreams? That they are an expression of our subconscious desires."

"Drop dead," I said flatly, and turned to go inside, my dignity in shreds.

Eugenia met me at the top of the first flight of stairs. "Oh, there you are, my dear," she said, smiling. "I was just wondering where you were."

"Philip and I went for a ride," I said.

"Kieran—you're just the lad I was wanting to see," Eugenia said. I knew without turning around that he had come up behind me, and I cringed. "Where's Philip?"

"Just coming," Kieran said.

Eugenia took Kieran's arm and drew him toward the parlor. "Have you lads been taking care of entertaining Selena whilst she's here with us?"

Kieran looked over at me, giving me a wickedly seductive smile. I quickly looked away. "I think you're asking the wrong person," he said. "Selena should know how well she's being entertained."

Philip entered at that moment, and Eugenia said, "Well, I don't know if you lads are aware, but the circus opens tonight in Wittcombe. I know Selena's been wanting to get out, and I thought this would be an excellent opportunity."

Kieran rolled his eyes.

"Aren't circuses exciting, luv?" Eugenia asked me, not having caught Kieran's look.

"I've never been to one," I admitted.

Eugenia appeared flabbergasted. "Never been to a circus! Well, you must go, my dear."

"Aye—nothing quite like ogling all the freaks," Kieran said with a look of obvious disgust.

"Now, Kieran, you know they don't do that anymore," Eugenia said crossly. "'Tis inhumane."

"We shall be happy to take Selena with us," Philip said gallantly. "Shan't we, cousin?"

"As you wish."

"Are you coming with us, Aunt Eugenia?" I asked.

"Oh, no. You young people will have so much more fun without some old biddy like me tagging along," Eugenia said with an airy laugh.

"'Twill be a smash, to be sure," Kieran muttered.

Eugenia went to fetch Derek and have him bring the car around while I went upstairs to change. When I came down, Eugenia told me that the others were waiting for me outside. Philip held the door open for me, and I slid into the back seat and bumped into Kieran. I felt a sudden shock as my hip and thigh smashed up against his, and quickly slid in the opposite direction. I'm sure Kieran noticed, because he was staring at me.

"Could you please move over a little, Selena?" Philip asked politely. "I haven't room."

I looked accusingly at Kieran, who shrugged elegantly and said, "I'm up against the door."

I tried to hide my consternation as I reluctantly slid closer to Kieran. Although he offered little in the way of conversation and kept his hands to himself, I was acutely aware of the nearness of Kieran's body the whole time we were in the car. I puzzled over his ability to fascinate and infuriate me at the same time, even when he wasn't doing anything.

Once again, I noticed how the citizens of Wittcombe cast their disapproving glances at the old Daimler. I wondered about this. Were the de Montforts unpopular, even resented, for some reason? Because they were well-to-do? Eccentric? Considered snobs? Perhaps they were known for not treating their servants very well, or grossly underpaying them. Perhaps it was the mere fact that they *had* servants.

Derek drove to the far side of town, where a large, colorful tent, and several smaller ones, were erected on a grassy plain. He parked the car and we got out. Kieran and Philip flanked me on either side as we headed for the ticket booth at the entrance of the largest tent. Philip paid for the tickets, while Kieran stood several feet away, eyeing the people who walked past. It suddenly struck me just how different Kieran was—standing there all alone, in his black velvet doublet and with his long, almost waist-length hair, he looked quite hopelessly out of place. It didn't seem so glaringly obvious at Cormoran, where everything was old, and not just Kieran's taste in clothes. Had you put a leather motorcycle jacket and a pair of jeans on him and dropped him off in Piccadilly Circus, most likely no one would give him a second glance; but here in Wittcombe, it was another story. I saw more than one person give him the evil eye as they walked past.

Philip led us to a trio of seats high up in the stands, and, to my puzzlement, the few people sitting near us all moved away. I knew that none of us smelled bad, and we certainly didn't have leprosy. I couldn't fathom their behavior.

Once the show started, Philip seemed to be enjoying himself. He continuously asked me whether I was having a good time as well; while on the other side of me, Kieran sighed with boredom, shifted uncomfortably in his seat, and finally excused himself, saying he'd be back shortly. I watched him make his way down the stands and disappear into the crowd.

"What's eating him?" I asked Philip.

"Oh, pay him no mind," Philip said flippantly.

"You always say that, but you never explain it," I pressed.

"How can anyone explain Kieran?" Philip said with a sigh. "You can't explain him. You just have to accept him. I'm sure you Americans have heard of the occasional eccentric Englishman? Well, you're related to one."

"Did he really go to Oxford? What did he study?"

"I don't remember. 'Twas a long time ago."

"It couldn't have been all that long ago. What is he—about my age?"

"Twenty-eight, I think."

"And how old are you—if you don't mind my asking?"

"Twenty-three."

"You're only twenty-three? But you seem so...mature."

"Old, you mean?"

"Oh, no, not at all. You know that wasn't what I meant. It's just that...you know so much. Did you ever go to college?"

"No, Kieran's the scholar of the family. I've always fancied myself as more of an adventurer. Aye, let Kieran have his books and his damned violin."

"You don't have any...ghosts or anything at Cormoran, do you?"

Philip seemed taken aback. "Ghosts? Whatever makes you say that?"

"It's just that—my first night here, I thought I saw a woman in white standing in my room—and then last night, I thought I saw this blue mist moving outside my window, but...well, I was probably just hallucinating. Kieran said he didn't see anything. He practically told me I was crazy."

Philip smiled as he placed a hand on my knee. "Selena, dear cousin, I can assure you, our fair castle houses no ghosts. If there were any stray spirits at Cormoran, I would think Kieran and I would know about it—we've lived there all our lives." He leant close to my ear and lowered his voice. "Never fear, my lady—I will protect you from whatever things go bump in the night, be they ghosts, blue mists, black cats, or my rapacious cousin."

My face flamed. I still wasn't certain I believed Kieran when he said he hadn't been in my bed, and Philip's remark seemed to confirm my suspicion. But I was too embarrassed to press the matter.

Kieran did not reappear until the show was over and Philip walked me outside. He materialized suddenly by my side, seemingly from nowhere, his face flushed.

"Are you feeling better, dear cousin?" Philip asked solicitously.

"Quite," Kieran said.

I wondered whether Kieran had wandered off to a pub, or perhaps to a clandestine meeting. I tried in vain to get a whiff of him as we rode in the car—surely he would have the smell of alcohol on his breath, or the traces of a woman's perfume on his skin—but there was nothing. I felt like making a casual inquiry, but didn't dare. I also was wondering what he had meant by his remark about "ogling all the freaks." Did that have anything to do with his disappearance during the performance?

Kieran was uncharacteristically taciturn on the way home. Once there, he headed straight for the music room, and a few moments later, I heard his violin.

"I'm rather hungry," I admitted to Philip. "I'm going to go to the kitchen and see if there's something I can nibble on."

Philip trailed me to the kitchen. I hadn't set foot in the kitchen before, so I had to look in every cupboard. "Where's the cook?" I asked. "Sissy, isn't it?"

Philip leant against a large wooden table in the center of the room. "She quit."

"When?"

"Today. I suppose Eugenia will have to hire someone new tomorrow."

I thought it rather funny that Philip referred to his mother by her first name, but if there was one thing I had learnt since my arrival at Cormoran, it was that there was nothing ordinary about this family. "I wonder why she quit," I said.

Philip shrugged. "Perhaps Kieran gave her a hard time once too often. It wouldn't be the first time he's scared off the hired help."

I remembered Sissy's look of annoyance when Kieran had rather curtly told her to fetch some more towels the other day. Perhaps that also explained why the de Montforts seemed none too popular in Wittcombe: Word had gotten around that they weren't the most agreeable of employers.

Philip stepped close to me, putting his hands on my hips and looking into my eyes. "If you would like to retire, my lady, I can escort you to your chamber."

"I wasn't thinking of going to bed this early," I admitted. "I'm really not tired."

A naughty, boyish smile spread across Philip's face. "I wasn't talking about sleeping," he said, with a roguish twinkle in his eye.

Perhaps I should mention at this point that ever since I was a teenager, I have had a weakness for men with long hair. My first real boyfriend was a guy named Steven James, whom I had dated when I was fifteen. Steven had long dark hair and two earrings in his left ear, and at the time I had thought he was just the coolest thing that ever walked upon the face of the earth. Whether it had started with him, or the various musicians on whom I had had the inevitable adolescent crush, or whether it had its roots even further back, in my childhood fixation with the Aztecs and various other Native American cultures, I really couldn't say. But it obviously worked to Philip's advantage, because his long, wavy hair, along with his heavy-lidded bedroom eyes and full lips, were impossible for me to resist, particularly when he pulled me close and began to kiss me.

"This is no place for a lady," he said huskily in my ear. "We can have more privacy and comfort in your chamber."

"Yeah," was all I was able to say.

Philip took my hand and led me across the moonlit inner ward to the gatehouse. As we climbed the stairs, I heard the strains of Kieran's violin. They seemed to follow us up, taunting me with the mournful strains of an old Irish tune, "Are Ye Sleeping, Maggie?" I stopped dead in my tracks. That tune had been an especial favorite of my mother. She had had an old vinyl record of someone playing that tune on a violin and had played it many times during her life. After her death, I remembered walking in on my father as he sat in his favorite armchair in the living room, listening to that record with tears streaming down his face. He later begged me to take the record away; he couldn't bear to listen to it anymore. I dug in my heels and resisted Philip's attempts to propel me up the stairs.

"What's wrong?" Philip asked.

"I know that song," I said distantly.

"'Tis only Kieran and his violin. Come on."

"Wait," I said.

"What is the matter?"

"Philip, I—" My head was swimming. I kept seeing Kieran's face, hearing his voice, feeling his touch. "I can't," I said in a tiny voice.

"Now, let's not hear any of this foolishness," Philip said, taking my arm.

I gently but firmly tried to pull away. "No, Philip, I mean it. I just can't."

A knowing smile spread across Philip's face. "You don't have to worry," he said gently. "I can't have children."

"Why not?" I asked, wondering why Eugenia had failed to mention this when she was bemoaning his unmarried state.

"I've had the mumps. It rendered me sterile. And I assure you, I don't harbor any sort of disease. You have nothing to fear."

"That wasn't really what I meant. Philip…I…I'm really terribly fond of you, I just…"

Philip just stood very still, an unreadable look in his eyes. "Be honest with me, Selena."

"I am being honest," I said.

"You certainly can't be that fickle—you couldn't get enough of me a moment ago, and now you don't even want me to touch you. There's someone else, isn't there?"

"No, Philip—"

"Don't lie to me, Selena."

"I'm not lying!" I don't know why it mattered so much to me that he not be angry with me.

"You don't know what you're getting yourself into, my lady. My cousin is not the sort of man you want to get mixed up with."

"I'm not 'mixed up' with him," I insisted.

"Trust me, Selena," he said softly. "I know what I'm talking about." He gently touched my cheek. "Won't you reconsider?"

"I just think I need some time," I said feebly. I turned and rushed back down to the second floor.

"Listen to your heart, Selena," Philip called after me. "You know that what we have together here is real. Don't allow yourself to be confused by a few notes on a violin or some fancy horsemanship."

I did not respond. I reached the music room and stopped in the doorway. Kieran was just coming to the last soulful note of the melody he was playing. He then slowly lowered his violin and turned to look me straight in the eyes.

"How did you know?" I asked.

"How did I know what, m'lady?"

"That that song was one of my mother's favorites."

Kieran looked quizzical. "And you think I knew this?"

"Somehow, I don't doubt it. You seem to know a lot more than you should. You really give me the creeps."

Kieran gave me his sardonic smile. "I don't believe 'creeps' is the right word for what I give you."

"I think that describes it exactly." I turned and went upstairs to my chamber.

That night I dreamt of a man making love to me, kneeling over me as in slow motion his torso straightened up and he threw back his head, sending his long mane of hair flying back off his face, and unleashed a loud, orgasmic groan…

A man with long black hair.

Chapter Six

The Waltz

I awoke in the morning to find daylight streaming in through the window, and with it came memories of the night before, rushing back in a sudden flood. I put my hand over my eyes and groaned. I felt guilty, and at first I could not fathom why. But as I puzzled over this, fleeting images began skidding across my mind, torturing me with the dreams I had had: Kieran, shirtless and soaked, kissing me in front of the parlor fireplace; Kieran astride me, making love to me with a primitive passion; Kieran caressing me as I lay in my bed. Philip simply could not compare with the touch of the man—either real or imagined—who had been in my bed the night before. How could I have given in so easily to Philip, when the man I burned for was his dark-haired cousin?

That question served only to pose another, perhaps even more confusing and disturbing: How could I desire Kieran when I didn't trust him—was even suspicious of him? I was at a loss to explain the strangeness of the whole situation.

I went downstairs to the Great Hall, feeling quite ravenous and wondering who would fix breakfast if the cook had quit. But my breakfast was already set out for me, and Derek was throwing another log in the fireplace.

"Good morning, Derek," I said as I sat down. "Who fixed breakfast today?"

Derek poked himself in the chest with an index finger.

I smiled at him and nodded. "It looks very good." Derek did not smile back; he merely inclined his head and left the room.

After I had eaten, I found Eugenia in the parlor. "Oh, hello, dear," she said, seeming distracted.

"What's the matter, Aunt Eugenia?"

"I had Derek post an advertisement in town for a new cook, but not even one person has arrived. What shall we do without a cook? Derek has too much to do as it stands already."

"Maybe none of the prospective cooks have cars to get out here," I suggested.

"I suppose I'll have to send Derek into town to try and find someone. Oh, dear."

"Aunt Eugenia, do you have the rest of the family tree?" I asked.

"Oh, yes, it's round here somewhere. I'll have to find it." She got to her feet. "Would you excuse me, luv? I'm afraid I don't feel well."

"Certainly, Aunt Eugenia," I said. "I hope you feel better soon."

I watched Eugenia leave the room and wondered if she were ill. She did seem to have a trace of pallor to her face. I wasn't certain what to do with myself until Philip got up, so I poked around in the parlor and, when I tired of that, I wandered into the music room and looked around. I have always had an insatiable curiosity regarding the lives of others—perhaps that's inevitable, considering my line of work—and my mother used to always say that one of these days it would get me into trouble. Still, I couldn't resist opening the two central doors on the sideboard and looking inside. I don't know what I had expected to find, but all that was inside was some rumpled sheet music and a couple of packages of violin strings. I closed the doors and opened the door to their right. Inside was a stack of letters and clippings which I carefully pulled out. I knew I was being dreadfully snoopy, but couldn't seem to help myself. A sick feeling settled in the pit of my stomach as I went through the stack.

On top was my letter to Eugenia, accepting her invitation for a visit. Beneath that were reviews of some of my books clipped from newspapers and magazines, and an article about me from the Atlanta Journal-Constitution. I wondered how on earth my relatives in England had gotten their hands on a newspaper from my hometown. There was even a photograph of me and a photocopy of my birth certificate. I thrust my hand back into the compartment and withdrew paperback copies of two of my novels. I sat on the floor, looking at the items in my hands as the feeling of uneasiness swelled into anger. To whom did these articles belong? I looked at the top of the sideboard: Kieran's wine decanter; Kieran's wine glasses; a stack of classical music CD's and a battery-powered CD player, also obviously Kieran's. And I didn't need to be told who in the household would have sheet music and violin strings. Had Kieran been collecting these things before I came? But the letter was to Eugenia. Had she been digging into my past more than she let on—or had it been Kieran, unbeknownst to Eugenia? And how had they gotten clippings from the Atlanta newspaper and a copy of my birth certificate? And what about my books? I wasn't even certain whether they were available in the United Kingdom.

Upon hearing approaching footsteps, I hastily shoved everything back into the sideboard and closed the door before leaping to my feet. It was only Ellen, who poked her head in the door and just as quickly withdrew. After she had left, I quickly went upstairs. Something about my discovery rankled me, but I knew I couldn't confront anyone about it, because then they would know I had been prying. I could almost hear my mother's voice saying, "Curiosity killed the cat."

I slowly walked the hallways upstairs, studying the doors. My room, Kieran's room, the bathroom, the water closet, Philip's room, Eugenia's room…and a mystery door. Obviously not having learnt my lesson, I turned the knob and pushed. It seemed to be a small storage room. I slipped inside and shut the door.

Sunlight filtered through the colored panes of a small, arched, stained-glass window, casting patterns of red, blue, green, and amber on the bare stone floor. The room was eerily quiet, and dust and mustiness hung in the air. In one corner stood a complete suit of armor; and beside it, leaning against the wall, was a large shield with an emblem of a black dragon spewing flame, much like the ones in the stained-glass windows in the dining hall. Several large wooden trunks sat in the room, some on top of each other, and scattered everywhere were the trappings of ages gone by: faded, folded-up tapestries; a spinning wheel, a baby's cradle; tarnished silver candelabra; a harp missing about half of its strings. I cautiously opened one of the chests, to find a wardrobe of neatly folded, magnificent gowns. I drew in my breath—I had never seen anything so beautiful, so antique, so priceless, even in a museum. I slowly reached out a hand to touch the exquisite fabric of the dress on top, scarcely daring to breathe. Perhaps I was afraid the dress would simply crumble away to dust under my fingertips.

"How did you get in here?"

Snatching my hand away, I jumped sideways and involuntarily screamed. Both hands flew to my mouth in fright.

"'Tis only I," Philip said.

I took my hands away from my mouth and said, "Don't do that to me! You scared me half to death!"

"I'm so sorry, my lady. I didn't mean to frighten you. But you shouldn't be in here by yourself. Something could fall on you…or there may be rats."

"I'm not afraid of rats," I said.

Philip walked over to the chest I had opened. He gently fingered the fabric of the top dress and murmured, "I'd almost forgotten about these."

"They're very beautiful," I said.

"Would you like to try one on?" Philip asked, pulling it out.

"I don't know whether I should," I said a trifle nervously. "I might wreck them."

"Rubbish. These gowns were made to be worn by a beautiful woman. And since their previous owners have no further use for them, I see nothing wrong with another beautiful de Montfort woman wearing them. They shall look much better on you than lying in that trunk." Philip pulled a couple more gowns from the trunk. "Which do you fancy?"

I chose a blue one and held it up to myself, but it looked too small. "I guess people were smaller back then," I said, disappointed. "I'm too tall. Probably none of these will fit me."

Philip dug further in the trunk and found a lovely ballgown from the early nineteenth century. It was of a pale, watery green silk with puffed sleeves, lace trim, and delicately embroidered garlands of flowers trailing down the front and around the hem and neckline. Philip held the gown up to me. "This one may do," he said. "Try it on."

"Hopefully, it belonged to a woman who was tall for her time," I said with a laugh as I accepted it. I took the dress and retreated behind a stack of boxes to change. I stripped down to my panties and slipped the dress over my head, but could not seem to manage the long row of tiny buttons up the back. I suddenly felt a pair of hands gently brush my hair to one side, over my left shoulder, and then glide down my sides to my waist.

"Do you need some assistance, my lady?" Philip asked softly, near my ear.

"I could, yes," I said in a very small voice, as he began to kiss my neck and the curve of my shoulder, which the gown's wide, deep neckline left exposed.

"You have very beautiful skin," he whispered, "and your scent is intoxicating." His hands seemed to caress me as they fastened the seemingly endless row of buttons. I looked down at myself. The gown had some extra room in the bust, but the waist fit and the length was about right. Philip gently arranged my hair so that most of it was once again falling down my back. "Let me see you," he said.

I turned around for his inspection. I watched his eyes slowly travel down my figure, and then back up again, taking in every detail. "You look stunning," he said. "That color looks splendid on you...especially with your eyes."

I laughed. "I'm afraid my eyes are nowhere near this color green."

"You look as though you should be holding court, my lady."

"I've always thought it would be fun to travel back in time for a day or two, just to see what it was like. I bet there was a lot going on here in the olden days, when the family was bigger. There were probably balls thrown here and wars fought."

"Indeed. The de Montforts of a few centuries ago were quite fond of dancing and carrying on, I understand. Quite a few balls were held in the Great Hall."

"Too bad we can't go back in time...just once."

"Why not?"

I blinked. "What?"

"Wear your dress, and we'll go down to the Great Hall now and give it a whirl. Kieran has a very fine compact disc player."

"I don't know how to dance," I said, embarrassed.

"I'll teach you. 'Tis quite easy, really."

Philip led the way downstairs, and stopped by the music room to pilfer Kieran's CD player and a couple of his CD's. Then he led me the long way around to the Great Hall, through a long corridor that went inside the castle walls. Ordinarily, I would have taken the shortcut through the inner ward. Perhaps Philip did not want us to be seen.

As I stepped through the door into the Great Hall, I marvelled once again at the room's size and stately grandeur. Shafts of sunlight shone through the windows on the west side, as the sun began to drop down on the horizon. Philip set the CD player on a tiny table at one end of the room and placed a CD inside it. I looked around me at the portraits of my ancestors on the walls. I could almost imagine them there in the room, watching me. The first notes from the "Vienna Blood Waltz" spilled forth from the CD player's speakers, and Philip turned up the volume. It seemed to echo in the high-ceilinged room.

Philip came and stood before me, placing his right hand on my back and taking my right hand in his left. "All you really are doing is moving round in a box," he explained. "Just follow what I do."

Philip made it sound so easy, but for some reason, I kept tripping over my own feet and bumping into him—either that, or I didn't move close enough, so that he ended up jerking me back to him. I laughed with embarrassment. "I have two left feet," I said.

"Nonsense," Philip said. "It just takes practice."

I had never learnt how to dance before—aside from the squaredancing I had been required to learn in gym class as a child—but I hadn't thought I would be quite so bad. Perhaps it stemmed from my embarrassment over the night before. I thought it odd that Philip made no mention of it. I was also thinking of my dream—of Kieran. My mind was in such a state of turmoil, I suppose it should have come as no surprise that I was having difficulty concentrating.

When the waltz ended, someone clapped; and a now-familiar, rusty voice said loudly, "Bravo!" I stopped and pulled away from Philip, spinning around to see Kieran leaning casually against the doorway, giving us a lazy, sardonic smile.

"Do you mind?" Philip said irritably.

Kieran walked over to the CD player and turned it off. "If our dear cousin wishes to learn how to waltz, 'twould be a good idea to take lessons from someone who truly knows how." He replaced the CD with another, and the first notes of Tchaikovsky's "Waltz of the Flowers" drifted through the room. Kieran casually walked up to me and said, in that elegantly mocking way, "May I have this dance, m'lady?"

I don't think I ever really answered him—I just stood looking into his unfathomable dark eyes as he took my hand in his and placed his other on my back, just below my shoulderblade, where it seemed almost to burn a hole through my dress. I was remembering the feel of a masculine hand gliding up my thigh and over my hip two nights before, and my face felt suddenly very hot. I wasn't really consciously aware of Kieran's voice instructing me on how to move my feet, but somehow his words must have sunk in, because in no time at all, we were gliding effortlessly across the room together. I was still marvelling at his selection—"Waltz of the Flowers," from *The Nutcracker*, has been one of my favorites since I was a little girl.

I was becoming hypnotized by Kieran's eyes. The room around us seemed filled with people, all dressed in fine nineteenth-century costume and all with their eyes on us. As the music got louder, the chandeliers overhead blazed with lights, laughter and lively voices mingled with the music, till everything around me became a blur of light, color, and sound. The only things I was sure of were the soaring notes of the music and the man who was holding me only a couple of inches away from him. I felt as though his eyes were reaching down into my soul. Suddenly, his hands were holding my face, cradling it gently in his long, slender fingers; and little by little he bent down, his eyelids gradually drooping and his mouth descending upon mine. I could do nothing but slowly drown in his kiss, tangling my fingers in his silky black hair and holding him close.

I came crashing back to reality as the waltz ended, and I realized Kieran's hands were still on my back and holding my right hand, exactly as they had been when we started. I quickly stepped back, pulling my hand off his right arm, and snatching my other hand from his. I sucked in great gulps of air, trying to catch my breath.

"That is how it is done," Kieran said, more to Philip than to me.

"If Selena wanted your services as a dance instructor, she would have asked for them," Philip said coldly.

Kieran cocked an eyebrow. "I wasn't aware of any protests on her part, cousin. Besides," he added, "you obviously aren't familiar with her favorite...composer." With that, he turned and strolled from the room. I looked over at Philip, who appeared to be silently fuming.

"Shall we try again?" I asked in a small voice, afraid Philip might also be angry with me for having allowed Kieran to cut in on him.

"No," Philip said, walking over to the CD player and turning it off. He turned to me and gave me his winsome smile. "Perhaps we should go somewhere where we'll have more privacy. Could I show you the way to my chamber, my lady?"

I didn't answer at first, as I was still staring at the doorway where Kieran had disappeared.

"Selena?" he prodded. "Are you with me?"

"I...I'm sorry, Philip. I think I need to lie down." And before he could protest, I fled the Great Hall and headed for my room.

I entered my room and quietly closed the door. Catching my reflection in the large mirror above the fireplace, I stepped closer to view myself in the dress. I didn't seem to be myself, and yet, I felt an eerie sense of *deja vu*. As I gazed into the mirror, I saw Kieran appear suddenly behind me, coming to stand so close that we were nearly touching. He gently brushed my hair to one side and placed his hands on my shoulders, which immediately burned from his touch. He bent his head and slowly began to kiss the curve of my neck. I quickly spun around, but no one was there.

"Kieran?" There was no sign of movement, and the door was still closed. I spun back around to look again into the mirror. I was alone.

I hastened to remove the dress and flung it over a chair. My heart pounded as I regarded it suspiciously. What was it about that dress? It seemed as though it were making me hallucinate, but of course I knew that was absurd. I threw some of my own clothes on and sat down to write Valerie a letter.

Dear Val,

I hope you got my first letter and that everything is going okay back home. How's my dad?

Something doesn't feel right here. I don't mean to alarm you, but there's a lot of weird things about this place that I can't explain. One night I found a black cat in my bed, and Philip and Kieran both said there's not any cats around here. Then I saw a woman in white who spoke to me and disappeared, and another night I saw a blue mist moving across the courtyard. I'm convinced it was the ghost again or something, but Kieran seems just as convinced that I'm crazy. I really do think he's up to something. I think he crawled into my bed one night and fondled me, but he denies it. Then he says I can't leave the castle grounds by myself. And in the sideboard where he keeps some of his stuff, I found two copies of my books and a bunch of clippings and stuff about me—including a photocopy of my birth certificate, of all things. I think maybe he knows more about me than he wants to let on, but I can't figure out why. He wants something out of me, I know that. I'm just not sure what it is, and it's driving me crazy. I don't dare talk to Philip or Eugenia about it, because they'll probably think it's nothing. And what makes it worse, I'm not sure how I feel about him. I don't trust him, but at the same time, I can't get him out of my mind. I'm so confused. I'm not sure of anything any more.

I'll see you in about a week, Val. Take care.

Love ya,

Sel

As I neared the end of my letter, I found myself growing drowsy and lay down on my bed, thinking I would just close my eyes and rest for a few minutes.

I stood in front of the fireplace in my bedroom, looking down at the front of the green ballgown, which I was wearing. A pair of strong, gentle hands were unbuttoning the back of the dress with excruciating slowness, and I heard words I knew I'd heard before, but now they were spoken in a different, huskier voice: "You have very beautiful skin, and your scent is intoxicating." I looked up, into the mirror, and saw Kieran's dark eyes staring at my reflection, the corners of his mouth curving into that coy little smirk with which I was becoming familiar; and I realized, for the first time, what that look really was—it was the look he was using to seduce me. Kieran let the dress fall to the floor, and I broke away from his gaze to look down and watch it fall—and I saw it was stained with copious amounts of blood. I screamed and woke up.

The room was dark, and moonlight shone through the open window. I hadn't realized I had been asleep so long. I sat up slowly, my heart still pounding from the dream I had had. I felt a sudden cold draft and thought I saw a flicker of candlelight in the corner of the room, near the door. "Hello?" I called. "Who's there?" There was no reply. "Eugenia? Kieran?" The light disappeared.

I stood on shaking legs and headed for the door. Opening it, I stuck my head out into the hallway and looked first left, then right. I thought I saw a flicker of light reflected against the stone walls disappearing around the corner. Leaving the door to my chamber open, I started down the hall after the light. It seemed to be heading in the direction of the stairs. When I reached the stairway, I looked down. I felt the cold draft again, making me shiver; but what made my shiver uncontrollable was the sight of an ethereal woman dressed in white disappearing around a bend in the stairs. I swallowed hard and started down after her. My knees were shaking but, somehow, I seemed to feel that this apparition would do me no harm.

"Hello!" I called. "Wait!"

The phantom woman stopped at the foot of the stairs and turned to look up at me, her candle in her hand. It was undoubtedly the same woman who had appeared by my bed my first night in the castle. She looked at me with large, melancholy eyes. I stopped where I was on the stairs, not daring to come any closer.

"Who are you?" I asked.

Slowly, her mouth opened, and she answered, "Sorrow." Then she turned and disappeared.

I hesitated but a moment before following her out the back door to the inner ward. She drifted over the cobblestones, leaving a dark stain on the ground before she vanished. I walked over the stain, which shimmered in the moonlight. It looked like blood. Then I turned and slowly looked up. Three stories directly above me was the window to my room. I turned and ran back inside, up the stairs to my room, and slammed the door. I dove under the covers of my bed and lay there the rest of the night, but I scarcely slept.

When the dawn light finally reached the dark recesses of my chamber, I got up from the bed, washed up and changed my clothes, then folded my letter to Valerie and sealed it in an envelope which I had addressed. Then I went downstairs to find Derek.

"Are you going into town today, Derek?" I asked him, when I finally found him, sweeping the kitchen floor. He nodded affirmatively. "Could I get you to do me a favor and mail this, please?" I asked. "I'd really appreciate it."

Derek took the letter from my hand and shoved it into the back pocket of his trousers. I furrowed my brow in concern, wondering whether he really intended to post it for me. But I didn't want to risk offending him, so I said only, "Thank you," and walked away.

As I passed the Great Hall, I suddenly remembered the carved wooden door that I had been unable to get open. I turned back and entered the Great Hall, heading straight for the door with its relief of flowers and vines. I tugged at the door again, but it refused to budge.

"My dear, whatever are you doing?" Eugenia's voice sailed across the room.

I quickly let go of the doorknob, jumping guiltily. "Oh, I...Just wondered where this went," I said lamely.

"Oh, that's just to the chapel. 'Tis fallen into such a state of disrepair, 'tis dangerous to even go in there. So we keep it locked, just in case someone might be inclined to go in and get hurt."

"What happened to it?"

"There was a fire in there several years ago. The damage was rather extensive, and we simply haven't the funds to have it repaired. I'm afraid our finances are in rather bad shape. This family's hit upon hard times, like nearly everyone else." She suddenly seemed to remember the young woman standing at her side. "My dear, this is Jane. She's going to be our new cook."

I looked at Jane, thinking that she was certainly better-looking than Sissy had been, or Ellen, and wondering whether Philip and Kieran had seen her yet. Immediately after that thought occurred to me, I wondered why I should care. Jane looked nearly the opposite of me: very fair shoulder-length blonde hair, dark eyes, very small-boned and petite. She had the sort of looks I would have envied when I was younger and more insecure. I wondered whether Kieran would give her a hard time, barking at her the way he had Sissy about the towels, or whether he might take advantage of his position over her and subject her to harassment of a more intrusive kind. I felt a prick of what must have been jealousy at such a thought and tried to brush it aside. What Kieran did should be of no concern to me, I tried to tell myself, without much success.

"Pleased to meet you," I told Jane.

"She can't hear you, luv. She's deaf-mute. But she *does* lip-read very well." Eugenia signed something to Jane, her hands fluttering rapidly.

Jane turned to me and smiled. Eugenia turned to me, taking care that Jane could not see her face. "I have such a soft spot for them, you know," she said lowering her voice. "The people in Wittcombe are so backward—no one wants to hire them, give them a chance." She sighed. "I do wish Kieran would learn sign language. He's so incredibly stubborn—he's worse than an old man."

I gave her a slightly ill smile but said nothing.

"Well, I must finish showing Jane the grounds. Philip should be home e'er long, my dear. And surely Kieran should be up soon. We'll talk later, if that's quite all right with you."

"Oh…sure," I said, and watched Eugenia and Jane depart. I gave one glance at the chapel door before walking away, as I suddenly remembered the clothes I had left in the storeroom. I went back to the gatehouse, upstairs to my room to retrieve the green gown from the chair where it lay. I looked out the window, wondering where Philip could have gone. He seemed to run a lot of errands. I left my chamber and headed for the storeroom, intending to put the gown back where I had found it. It simply wouldn't do to leave something like that lying around, I told myself.

But when I tried the storeroom door, I found it to be locked. I pounded on it in frustration, when suddenly a voice behind me asked, "Having some difficulty, m'lady?"

I spun around to find Kieran's eyes on me. He looked slightly amused, probably having had a good laugh to himself over my pathetic attempts.

"The door's locked, and I was going to put this away." I indicated the dress. "I also…um…left my clothes in there."

"I'll get the key," Kieran said, and disappeared. He returned a moment later with a large, slightly rusty, iron key, one of those extremely archaic types that one instantly recognizes as a key, but that no one uses any more to actually open anything. As I watched Kieran deftly unlock the door, I wished to myself that he would stop sneaking up on me all the time. It seemed as though he were bent on giving me heart failure.

With a quick twist of the wrist, Kieran turned the knob and pushed the door open. "There you are, m'lady," he said as he held the door for me. "And how else might I be of service?"

"You needn't, thank you," I said, brushing past him.

He followed me into the room anyway and watched me fold up the gown. Knowing that he was standing there watching me, and that I was in the room alone with him, made me nervous, and my hands shook slightly as I folded up the garment.

"I don't know whether I told you how beautiful you looked in that yesterday," he said, his voice very low.

"No…you didn't," I said, my hands shaking even more than before.

"*Very* beautiful," he said, his voice dropping a couple more decibels, so that I could just barely hear him. His hands began to help mine fold the dress. "It suits you much better than trousers."

"I'm comfortable in trousers," I said in a small voice I scarcely recognized as my own.

Kieran finished folding the dress and replaced it in one of the trunks. I studied his profile, feeling a strange, fluttery sensation as I looked at him. "Where did you learn to dance?" I asked, simply to be saying something.

"'Tis been a lifelong pursuit," he said, not looking up.

"You're very good," I said weakly.

Kieran turned then and looked at me. "Is that a compliment, m'lady?"

"Of course it is," I said, wondering what he was getting at.

"Good. Because 'tis the first one I believe I've heard from you since the night we met, when you praised my musical abilities."

I knew I had to get out of that room. I kept thinking of my daydream, or hallucination, or whatever it was, from the day before, of Kieran's taking me in his arms and kissing me as we waltzed. Suddenly the room felt stiflingly hot, and seemed to spin a little.

"I have to go," I said, gathering up my clothes. I headed for the door.

"I don't suppose there are any ghosts in *Philip's* chamber," Kieran's voice said snidely from behind me. I froze. "Or any black cats?"

Slowly, I turned around and faced him. "I wouldn't know."

Kieran nodded, giving me the same look he had that day on our ride through the forest, when he had seemed unconvinced when I told him that I had had only a bad dream. "Sometimes," he said ominously, "we fear the wrong things."

I made no reply, but simply turned and left the room on legs that suddenly seemed unsteady.

Chapter Seven

The Duel

I found Philip down by the stables a few minutes later. "Oh, good, you're back," I said, relieved. I didn't want to have to think about Kieran.

Philip seemed to have forgotten about the previous day. "Forgive me for rushing off this morning, but I had some legal papers to pick up. I had quite forgotten about them."

"Oh, that's quite all right. I forget things all the time."

"Would you like to ride today? 'Tis rather cloudy, but I don't think it will rain—not for a while, anyway."

"Okay," I said.

Philip had Ellen saddle our horses, and he helped me mount. As we headed outside the castle walls, I asked him, "Why didn't you wake me? I would have gone with you into town."

"You would have been quite bored, I will assure you."

"But I like to get out once in a while, too. The only time I've been to town was when we went to the circus, and then we came straight home."

"I'm sorry, my dear. I fear we are from two different worlds. You are from the city, with its flashing lights and crowds of people, whilst I am used to a slower, much simpler lifestyle, one of leisure and simple pleasures, unhampered by all your modern-day hustle and bustle. Things have changed little over the years at Cormoran."

I was puzzled. I thought he had described himself as an "adventurer" a couple of days before, but I decided against pointing this out. "Yes, I noticed that," I said instead. "It's like this place was caught in a time warp. I should use it for the setting of a story."

"And what kind of story would that be?"

"I don't know yet."

Philip gave me his winning smile. "I hope you'll let me read it after you've written it. I'm so looking forward to reading your stories."

From this remark, I gathered that Philip did not know about the two books in the sideboard. That left Kieran and Eugenia. I kept thinking about Kieran, wondering what made him tick. I thought about questioning Philip about him, but realized that I probably brought Kieran's name up too often already; and Philip was already getting jealous. My mind refused to drop the subject, however, and as a result, I was distracted, unable to really focus on anything that Philip said to me for the rest of our ride.

When we returned to the castle, Ellen took our horses and led them back to the stable, and Philip led the way to the Great Hall. "I can't remember if I returned Kieran's CD player," Philip said. "I must have left it in the Hall."

I followed Philip into the Great Hall and stopped in my tracks once inside. Kieran was at the far end of the room, a fencing foil in one hand. His shirt was mostly open, as though perhaps he had been practicing by himself and become a little warm, though I saw no evidence of sweat on his face or chest. Even though I was several feet away from him, I thought I detected that wicked gleam in his eye as he cocked his head and said, "*Cousin,*" in an ominous, almost threatening tone. "You're just in time." Using his sword, he made a sweeping gesture towards the rack from which he'd apparently taken it.

"My pleasure," Philip said, striding over to the rack and removing a foil of his own. When Kieran saw that his kinsman was ready, he placed one hand elegantly on his hip as he and Philip crossed blades.

"I shall look forward to besting you yet again," Kieran said with a sardonic smile.

"Then you shall have a long wait," Philip retorted, making his attack. Kieran easily defended himself, and the ring of steel upon steel echoed hollowly in the long, high-ceilinged room. I found their duelling quite exciting to watch, as alternately one lunged and the other parried, both men obviously being accomplished fencers. I noted the difference in their styles: Kieran's movements were graceful and elegant, as though carefully choreographed; while Philip's were solid and decisive, calculated to waste no movement. Back and forth they moved across the floor, seeming so evenly matched that surely this duel would end in a draw. As Philip sought to gain the upper hand, he caught the tip of his blade on the wide swath of lace that edged one side of Kieran's partially unbuttoned shirt front, running it through one of the little holes in the lace. As though in slow motion, Kieran looked down at Philip's blade, slowly looked up, fixing the other man with his dark stare and, with a snarl, suddenly ripped his shirt free and spun around in a complete circle, knocking Philip's foil from his hand and sending it spinning across the room, where it clattered to the floor. He lunged at Philip, who lost his footing and fell to the floor. Kieran held the tip of his blade carefully at Philip's throat, just barely touching his Adam's apple.

"You," Kieran hissed, "owe me a shirt."

Philip scrambled backward, twisting and sliding across the floor to grab his sword. "This isn't over yet, *cousin,*" Philip said as he got to his feet. The clink of steel rang out once again as Philip tried to back Kieran into a corner. With a snap of his wrist, Kieran sent the foil flying from Philip's hand and made a thin gash across his face, from which a line of bright red blood appeared. Kieran pushed past Philip, casting a smug little smile at him as he leisurely strode over to the far side of the room. Enraged, Philip snatched a heavy broadsword from a rack on the wall close at hand and descended upon his kinsman, swinging his sword with both hands as though he meant to take off Kieran's head.

"*Kieran!*" I shrieked, horrified. He turned at the exact moment that I screamed, leaping out of the way of the blade. He dashed over to the rack from which Philip had taken the sword, seizing another very much like it and turning to Phillip with a savage snarl, his eyes seeming to set off sparks.

"Come and fight like a man," Philip taunted him.

Kieran held his own using the larger sword but clearly was not as comfortable with it. Philip, on the other hand, seemed to be in his element. Kieran tried backing him against a wall, but Philip placed a foot squarely on his abdomen and pushed him away. Kieran stumbled back, his sword dropping to one hand. Philip took the offensive, bearing down on Kieran, who tried to extend his sword but wasn't fast enough. He fell backwards to the floor, and Philip took the stance that Kieran had only moments before, the point of his sword poking at the other man's throat.

"Do you yield?" Philip demanded.

Kieran lay panting for a moment, his eyes narrowed and brimming with hatred. "No!" he spat out suddenly, kicking Philip in the groin. Philip dropped his sword and fell to his knees, clutching the bruised area, and Kieran jumped to his feet. Philip quickly recovered and lunged at Kieran's back, tackling him around the waist and knocking him to the floor. They scuffled around like a couple of boys in a schoolyard, and when Philip got his hands around Kieran's throat, as though he meant to choke the breath from him, I decided I'd had enough.

"Stop it!" I cried. "Stop it, both of you!" I didn't want to admit how much it bothered me to see what had started out as a civilized duel collapse into such a primitive brawl.

Philip got to his feet, instantly apologetic. "We didn't mean to offend you, dear cousin." He walked over to me, taking my hands in his and looking into my eyes. "Sometimes we just forget ourselves, that's all. Come, let's have a drink." He let go of my hands and headed for the doorway. As he was about to reach it, out of the corner of my eye I saw Kieran rising to his feet as he pulled a dagger from his right boot and hurled it at Philip's retreating form.

"Look out!" I screamed as the dagger imbedded itself in the door frame. Philip slowly turned, cocking an eyebrow at Kieran.

"You missed," he said dryly.

Kieran inclined his head, smiling sardonically. "On the contrary, *dear* cousin," he said, his voice low, "I hit my intended target exactly."

A slow smile spread across Philip's face, and he began to laugh. The lines of Kieran's face began to relax, and he looked as though he might actually laugh, too.

"I don't think that was very funny," I said, unamused.

"Oh, come now, we're only having a bit of fun," Philip said.

"I think you guys must be pretty sick when your idea of 'fun' is nearly killing each other."

"Selena, my dear," Philip said, "we could never kill each other. We can anticipate each other's actions too well. Besides—we're family."

"*My* family never acted like that," I said indignantly.

"My lady," Kieran said, "we *are* your family."

I turned and attempted to stalk from the room. Since I chose to use the doorway at the opposite end of the room from the one where Philip stood, I had to pass Kieran. He stepped in front of me to block my path and looked intently into my eyes as he lowered his voice and said, "I'm honored by your concern for my safety, m'lady." I wasn't certain what I saw there in his eyes, but it sent a weird tingle down my spine.

"Don't be," I said archly as I stepped around him. "And I'm not your lady." I turned to leave.

"Selena, wait!" Philip called. I reluctantly turned around. Philip hastened over to me but stopped when he reached Kieran. "Don't walk away angry. We meant no harm. Come—let us eat and have a few drinks," Philip said, putting an arm around Kieran's shoulders. "Won't you join us, my lady?"

I relented when I saw the earnest look on Philip's face. I *was* tired of eating alone. "All right," I said, and followed them to the dining hall.

Jane was just setting the table as we walked in. Philip signed to her, with what I assumed must have been a request for three place settings. Jane set the places and then produced a bottle of wine from a liquor cabinet in the corner of the room, which she poured into each of our wine goblets. As Jane left the room, Philip got to his feet and lifted his goblet in a toast.

"To family," Philip said. "To those ties which can never be severed."

"Hear, hear," Kieran said as he raised his wine goblet and then quickly downed its contents. I took a sip from mine as I watched Kieran reach for the bottle and pour himself some more. "Where's our dinner?" he bellowed without even looking up.

"She can't hear you—she's deaf," Philip said.

Kieran scowled. "Why can't Eugenia hire someone who can bloody *hear*?"

"Probably so they don't have to listen to your incessant complaints," Philip said smoothly. Kieran only glared at him.

Jane re-entered the room, wheeling before her a cart laden with food. The first thing she placed on the table was a very large roast, which looked big enough to be nearly half a cow. Kieran eyed the roast critically as he picked up a large knife and a meat fork and began to carve a thick slice. His look of disgust deepened as the piece of meat was separated from the remainder of the roast, and he held it out at arm's length, dangling on the end of the meat fork.

"What do you call *this*?" Kieran demanded, giving his arm a jerk and making the meat flap only inches from Jane's face. She just stood staring at him, her eyes looking as though they had grown about four sizes larger.

"It looks like a piece of meat," Philip quipped.

"'Tis virtually burnt to a crisp," Kieran said, ignoring Philip. "I want my meat *rare*. I want there to be *blood* when I cut it. Do you see any *blood* here?"

"She can't hear you," Philip said again.

"She can bloody *lip-read*, can she not?" Kieran demanded, flipping the slice of meat so that it came off the fork and nearly slapped Jane in the face.

"What is *wrong* with you?" I cried, appalled. "No wonder you can't keep servants around here!"

"Take this out of here immediately," Kieran told Jane, "and bring me some real food." She made no move, but simply stood there, shaking. With a growl, Kieran shoved the platter roughly across the table, so that it went sailing into the air and landed on the floor with a crash. Jane ran from the room.

"Honestly, cousin," Philip said, getting up to retrieve the other dishes from the serving cart. He passed me some potatoes and carrots, but suddenly I seemed to have lost my appetite. I looked across the table at Kieran pouring himself some more wine.

"If this is what you're like after one or two drinks, I'd hate to see you really drunk," I said.

"I don't get drunk," Kieran said loftily.

"That's what they all say."

Kieran poured some more wine into my goblet. "Drink up, cousin."

Jane tiptoed back into the room with another, much smaller, roast, which she gingerly set in front of Kieran, her hands trembling noticeably. Kieran eyed the meat for a moment before cutting into it. Blood seeped out and nearly flooded the platter.

"Now that's a roast," Kieran said, placing the slice on my plate. I looked down at it and felt like throwing up. Kieran next flipped a couple of thick slabs onto Philip's plate and then a couple more on his own.

"How can you eat that?" I asked, nauseated. "It's practically raw."

"It's an acquired taste," Kieran said flippantly, then turned to Jane. "More wine."

Jane beat a hasty retreat as Kieran attacked the slab of meat on his plate. She returned a moment later with another bottle of wine. Kieran poured himself some, took a drink, and spit it out as if he had been poisoned.

"You call this wine?" Snatching up the bottle, he pitched it into the fireplace, where the bottle smashed into a thousand tiny shards and the flames leapt up dangerously high. "What in bloody hell is this?"

I got to my feet. "I've had enough. I wouldn't accept all the money in the world in exchange for eating with you. Your table manners are atrocious."

"Aye, and my bedroom manners are even worse," Kieran agreed, with a wicked gleam in his eye.

"You're a fucking animal," I said, and left the room. I heard Philip call my name, and Kieran, his voice now calm, saying, "Let her go."

***

I really didn't want to spend the rest of the evening in my room, so after fuming and feeling indignant for about an hour, I quietly opened the door and stepped out into the hallway, with the intention of going downstairs. As I passed Kieran's room, I heard voices coming from within, and I stopped to listen.

The first voice I heard was unmistakenly Kieran's—I'd know his voice anywhere. "You needn't bother," he said.

"And who are you to tell *me*?" It was Philip's voice. "Just because you went to Oxford, you think you're so much more bloody intellectual than everyone else. You can put on airs all you wish, cousin, but you'll never erase the fact that you're a bastard."

I was startled. I hadn't known that Kieran was illegitimate.

"You've always been jealous of me," Kieran said. "You've always felt that you had to compete with me. Well, this is one competition you won't win, cousin. You de Montforts be damned. The future of this family lies with the Ramseys."

"By that, I suppose you mean Selena and yourself?"

"You won't allow yourself to see the obvious. Selena's heart has made a choice—and 'tis not you, cousin."

"Still the same old Kieran. Arrogance and conceit were always your greatest virtues."

I couldn't bear to hear any more, so I fled downstairs. I was mortified. Were Philip and Kieran competing for me? Was this all some sort of game for them, toying with my feelings? I could believe it of Kieran, but Philip? What a performance he had put on, and I had fallen for it completely. I was mad at myself for not having known better. I decided at that moment that they were both total cads.

I went into the music room and walked past the harpsichord to a magnificent piano I had noticed in the corner of the room. I gingerly sat down on the bench and opened the cover over the keyboard. I fingered a couple of keys—it was in perfect tune. It had been a long time since I had played, and I thought I would surely be quite rusty. I tried playing Beethoven's *Für Elise*, which had always been one of my favorites. It came out awkwardly at first, but in a matter of minutes I found I was playing as though I had never stopped. I was startled and dismayed when Philip appeared in the doorway a few minutes later, and I jumped and missed a note when he spoke.

"There you are, Selena."

"Go away. I don't want to talk to you," I said, returning to my playing. I glanced over my shoulder to see Philip take a couple of steps into the room, and Kieran appeared in the doorway behind him. "And I *really* don't want to talk to *you*."

"I'm sorry if we offended you," Philip said gently. "Please accept our apologies."

"I don't want apologies. I want people to be honest with me."

"She was listening at the door," Kieran said flatly.

Philip came and stood by my side. "You heard—? Selena, it wasn't what it sounded like. Please believe me."

I stopped playing and regarded Philip silently. I wanted so much to believe him but didn't know whether I dared. I wondered whether Kieran was just very astute, or whether I had somehow given myself away.

Kieran approached the piano bench and lowered himself to one knee. "If m'lady will forgive my behavior, I shall see to it personally that the rest of your stay is most enjoyable," he offered, the picture of perfect chivalry. "And you're quite right—I turn into a perfect beast when I drink. 'Tis one of my human failings, I'm afraid."

In spite of myself, I couldn't help but be charmed by Kieran's contrite look and manner. The contrast between his attitude now and at dinner was like Dr. Jekyll and Mr. Hyde. My anger at him seemed to slowly melt away as I thought of his teaching me to dance, helping me fold up the antique gown, serenading me with his violin. I looked into his dark, unfathomable eyes and felt my breath catch in my throat. There was no denying that Kieran was the most irresistible man I had ever met—even though he had a knack for making me absolutely furious with him. At least he was man enough to admit he had a drinking problem, and that was a start.

"The apologies are accepted," I said.

Kieran sat beside me on the piano bench. "Don't let me interrupt you, m'lady," he said. He was so close as to be almost touching.

"Perhaps you would play something for us," I suggested. "I'm sure you're a much better pianist than I."

"I have simply practiced more," Kieran said, picking up the tune where I had left off. "You've neglected the piano, more than likely to get back at your parents for refusing you the violin."

I marvelled at Kieran's assessment of the situation. I had never thought about it before, but I had the nagging feeling that he was right. How did it always seem that he had his finger ever on my pulse?

I slid down on the piano bench to give Kieran more room. My heart pounded as I watched his fingers nimbly dancing over the keys. In Kieran's skilled hands, Beethoven's music took on an intoxicating sensuousness I had never felt before. Was there anything he couldn't play?

By the time Kieran reached the last tender note, I was feeling dizzy and short of breath, and my heart was pounding painfully against my ribs. I involuntarily put a hand to my chest.

"Are you ill?" Philip asked suddenly, his face showing fearful concern.

"It must be something I ate," I said quickly. "It's giving me heartburn, I think."

"You didn't eat anything, m'lady," Kieran said, eyeing me.

The room seemed to grow stiflingly hot all of a sudden, and began to spin. I stood up, took one step, then twisted and nearly slumped to the floor, all in slow motion, or so it seemed; but a pair of arms caught me before I could collapse completely and slam my head on the floor.

I had always thought that when a person fainted, they lost consciousness, and surely that was what I should have done. But somehow I was aware of voices, of touch, of the arms that held me.

"She's fainted," I heard Philip's voice saying, as though very far away.

"Let's take her upstairs," Kieran's voice replied, equally distant. I was dimly aware of being lifted by someone's arms; and I don't know how I knew, but I was certain in my mind that it was Kieran. This puzzled me, because I couldn't, even later, figure out how he could pick me up and carry me as though I were a child, when he was scarcely bigger than I. He carried me up the winding stairs to my room, where he laid me on my bed; and, even through my fog, my whole body seemed to be on fire from his touch.

"Don't even think about it," I heard Philip say.

"Really, cousin—what do you take me for?" Kieran replied.

"That which you said yourself—a beast."

Kieran gave a dry, almost nefarious laugh. "What are you afraid of—*cousin*?"

I heard the door close none too gently, and then I passed into total oblivion.

***

I slept fitfully, haunted by disturbing dreams. The most vivid of these started out as an echo of an event from the day before, when Kieran had taught me how to waltz. I could hear the music sweeping us through the room and see the chandeliers blazing overhead and the last rays of the evening sun filtering through the arched windows on the west side of the Great Hall. Everything around me became a blur, as I could focus only on the man who held me close. I could feel the nearness of his body, his strength, the sweetness of his lips as he began to kiss me. For a moment, he held my face in his hands; but then, slowly, they began to slither downward, down my neck, across my shoulders and down my arms, pushing the gown, which left most of my shoulders already exposed, down even further. Then I felt his hand at my back, unfastening my dress, as his mouth travelled downward in the direction his hands had already taken. I tangled my fingers in his hair, shivering with exquisite anticipation as his lips blazed a trail to my breast. I couldn't keep from crying out as I held him tight. The next moment, he was easing me down onto the pile of our discarded clothes on the floor, where our bodies seemed to become entwined. He caressed me with his hands, his lips, his tongue, arousing me far beyond anything I had felt before. I couldn't remember ever wanting a man so very badly, knowing that I *had* to have him, so that when at last I felt him gently part my thighs, poised to enter me, I couldn't stop myself from crying out his name.

I awoke with a start. Had I really called Kieran's name out in my sleep? I began to relax, thinking it only part of my dream, when I heard a soft rap at the door. It slowly opened a few inches, and Kieran's face revealed itself from behind it. "You called, m'lady?"

"No, I didn't," I said, trying to hide my embarrassment. "You can go back to bed."

A conspiratorial smile slowly spread across Kieran's face, and he got that wickedly seductive look in his eye. I realized, to my mortification, that this was not a man who could be easily fooled. He must have heard his name more plainly than I had thought. Slipping all the way into the room, he quietly closed the door behind himself.

"And just what do you think you're doing?" I asked, trying to swallow the lump in my throat and sound indignant.

Kieran just stood looking at me with that gleam in his eye. "I know what I heard," he said.

"And I said it's nothing," I insisted. "You may go back to bed now."

"I may," Kieran replied, "but I won't."

"What do I have to do—scream?"

"You've done that once already, m'lady," Kieran said with an infuriating little smile, "and as you can see, *I* am the only one who responded."

"That's because—" I was about to say, "because it was your name," but I stopped myself. Kieran seemed to have picked up on my train of thought, however.

"So if you scream again, no one will come, because they shall assume you are only getting what you want."

I glared at him. "Get out of here. *Now.*"

Kieran made no move to leave.

"Perhaps you didn't hear me clearly," I said. "I said I want you to leave."

"Aye, I heard you indeed. I also heard you tonight when you called me 'a fucking animal.' Rather an amusing little double-entendre, is it not?"

"No, it is not," I retorted. "Because I only meant one thing when I said that, and that is that I found your performance at the dinner table tonight most revolting."

Kieran cocked an eyebrow. "Is it really?"

"I'll scream for Philip," I threatened as Kieran approached the bed.

Kieran shook his head. "Philip...you really can't count on him, you know, my dear cousin. He's actually quite unreliable. Who came to your aid when you thought you saw a ghost? Who caught you tonight when you fainted?"

"If you think I'm going to trust *you,* you'd better think again."

"One of these days, Selena, you are going to find out the truth—and you're not going to like it. But then again," he added, raising his eyebrows as though a thought had just struck him, "perhaps you will."

Chapter Eight

The Portrait

I slept very little after Kieran left. I was up nearly at the crack of dawn; I washed up and got dressed and headed downstairs to the parlor. Not even the servants were up yet, so I rummaged through the parlor bookshelves. Not finding what I was looking for, I moved on to the music room. After nearly turning the place upside down and still coming up empty-handed, I tried the library. I had to find the rest of that family tree, and Eugenia had seemed somewhat reluctant to supply it. I kept hearing Kieran's voice saying, "*One of these days, Selena, you are going to find out the truth—and you're not going to like it. But then again...perhaps you will.*" I thought of the looks the citizens of Wittcombe gave the de Montforts' black Daimler...Kieran's refusal to let me leave the premises without him or Philip...Eugenia's penchant for hiring only mute servants...the blue apparition in the courtyard and the ghostly woman in white...and the previous night had been most disturbing. First there had been Kieran's appalling lapse in manners; his diet, which seemed to consist of only red wine and equally red—and bloody—meat; and the bizarre malady which had struck me for no apparent reason. And for some weird reason, I kept having dreams about Kieran that grew steamier with each successive night. I knew there was definitely something wrong with this family, and I intended to find out what it was—whether I liked it or not. And I had a feeling the family tree might yield my first clue.

I pulled a book out of one of the bookshelves, and stuffed behind it was a yellowed, folded-up piece of paper. Snatching it from its hiding place, I rushed over the desk and flattened the paper as best I could. It was the second portion of the family tree! I looked at the bottom and saw that the last dates were from around 1800, so I figured there had to be one more part. I started back up at the top and worked my way down, scanning all the names. One name seemed to jump out at me, and for a moment I thought my heart had stopped:

Kieran Ramsey
b. 1575 d. 1604

No names were connected below it, so apparently he had died leaving no children. I also noticed that no woman's name was joined beside him, so he must not have ever married, either. I remembered Eugenia's saying that Kieran was "an old family name," so surely this was just an ancestor with the same name. On the other hand, there were no other Kierans on either of the parts of the family tree that I had seen, and I suddenly remembered Philip's telling me that Kieran had had a brother and two half-sisters, now deceased. With an overwhelming feeling of dread, I noticed that the Kieran Ramsey born in 1575 had also had a brother and two half-sisters.

I slowly sank down into the desk chair. I could neither describe nor explain the horribly creepy feeling that came over me, or why I suddenly jumped up and ran upstairs to get my camera. Returning to the library, I took a photograph of the chart and then I felt a strange lure that led me to the music room, to the door on the far side of the room that I had seen before but not yet tried. I just stood there staring at it for what seemed an interminable moment, feeling something beckoning to me to open the door, but scared nearly half to death at the thought of what I might find on the other side.

"...you're not going to like it. But then again...perhaps you will."

I put my shaking hand upon the doorhandle. The door did not give way easily, causing me to think that perhaps all the moisture in the air had caused it to expand. I remembered a closet door in my parents' house that had done that—every time there was a lot of rain, the door became hard to open. I turned the handle again and pushed very hard, and the door swung open this time. I found myself in another room roughly the size of the music room, strewn about with heavy-looking chairs with faded upholstery and an assortment of small occasional tables. A shield with a coat of arms identical to the one I had found in the storage room hung over the fireplace, and the walls were hung with more large portraits in heavy gilt frames, like those in the Great Hall. I slowly walked around the room, looking at each one in turn. I observed that there were more portraits here of women and children, though there were a couple of men as well. I came upon one of these and stood staring at it in a state of shock.

It was a portrait of a young man in about his late twenties, dressed in a jade green doublet with a white shirt collar and a large swath of lace showing at the neck. His long black hair was swept back off his face, with several carefully coiffed locks cascading over his left shoulder in soft waves. He stood with the knuckles of one hand placed elegantly upon his hip, his other hand holding a rapier pointed at the floor. It was difficult to appraise his physique, with his doublet's exaggerated shoulders and peplum waist; but there was no mistaking those dark, hypnotic eyes; that long, aristocratic nose; or the sensual lips with their coy little smirk. I knew that face well.

Slowly, I brought my camera up to my eye and snapped a photo of the painting. Just as the flash went off, a voice from behind me made me jump.

"So, I see you found the rest of the portraits."

I spun around, my heart in a state of near-paralysis, to see Kieran standing in the doorway, dressed as was his custom in a white, lace-edged shirt, black trousers, and black riding boots. He slowly walked over to the painting I had been studying, standing beside it and folding his arms, as though daring me to make a comparison. He even offered me the same facial expression as the portrait.

"That's you, isn't it?" I asked, in a voice so tiny, it was scarcely audible.

Kieran turned and looked at the portrait as though he had expected it to have changed in the last two minutes. He looked back at me. "'Tis a fair likeness, it is not?"

"Why…I mean…when…?" My head was spinning. That painting *had* to have been done recently if it was of Kieran, hadn't it? Yet, it looked as old and timeworn as the other paintings around it. And then there was the matter of the Kieran Ramsey on the family tree, a Kieran Ramsey who had been born in 1575 and died in 1604. Those dates seemed to coincide with the style of dress in the portrait, as far as I could tell. "I don't understand," I said blankly.

Kieran leant back against the wall. "What don't you understand?"

"Why that painting looks so much like you. It *can't* be you—can it?" Kieran made no response. "*Can* it?" I repeated.

"How else might you account for the amazing likeness? You don't see any portraits of *your* double round here, do you?"

"I'm not aware of my having a double."

"And neither do I. Not even my late brother looked so much like me."

"So when was that painted?"

"If memory serves me correctly—1603."

I just stared at him. "That's impossible."

Kieran cocked an eyebrow. "Is it?"

"That would make you over four hundred years old!"

Kieran put a hand to his chest. "Please, dear cousin, you make me feel *ancient*."

"You'd better not tell me you've been reincarnated, because I won't believe it."

"All right, I won't. And 'twould be the truth, because I am the only Kieran Ramsey, unlike all the Philip de Montforts."

"The Kieran Ramsey on the family tree died in 1604."

"Yes, one year after this painting was finished. Tragic, is it not?"

"It's impossible," I said again.

Kieran slowly walked over to where I stood, stopping only a few inches away. My heart raced at the nearness of him, and my mouth felt dry.

"Search your feelings," he said, his voice very low. "You know what I am."

"You're not a ghost. I know that much."

"No, I am not a ghost. Ghosts do not have flesh...and *blood*." He placed particular emphasis on this last word, staring deep into my eyes.

"No," I said in horror. "That's not possible."

"You know it is. Why else would you fear me?"

"I don't fear you."

"You don't?" Kieran slowly reached inside his shirt and pulled out two envelopes. "Then why should you *needlessly* alarm your friend back in the States?"

I looked down at the top letter he held, at Valerie's name and address written out in my own hand. The envelopes were ripped open along their tops, obviously having been opened and read.

"Where did you—how dare you—!" I didn't finish either sentence; I simply flung myself at him, trying to snatch the letters from his hand and hit him in the process. He grabbed my arms and held me fast with what seemed a superhuman grip, and the letters fluttered to the floor.

"You don't know what you're doing," he said. " 'Tis useless to fight, Selena. You cannot win."

"Then I'll die trying."

"What do you think I would do to you, m'lady? If I wanted to drink your blood, don't you think I would have done so already?"

"How do I know you haven't—when you slipped into my bed that one night and then tried to convince me the next day that I was only dreaming?"

Kieran gave me an evil smile. "I would have left teethmarks." He released my arms. "You never exactly pushed me out."

"What do you mean, *never*? You were there more than once?"

Kieran just gave me his infuriatingly smug little smile.

"You disgust me!" I exclaimed.

"You're not a very good liar, m'lady." Kieran's smile turned wicked. "If I disgust you, why do you persist in concocting your lurid little fantasies about me?"

"I don't!" I cried, feeling as though my very soul had been stripped bare, and I could find nothing with which to clothe myself.

"I know what you think…what you feel," Kieran said, his voice scarcely more than a whisper. "I know the dreams that you dream. I'm a part of you, Selena. We share the same blood." He fixed me with those hypnotic eyes. I could sense in them the promise of untold dangerous delights; I was acutely aware of a primeval eroticism lurking beneath his cool, dignified surface, waiting to burst forth…perhaps waiting for me.

"You can't be a vampire," I said weakly.

"And why is that?"

"You get up during the day…you can eat and drink…" I suddenly remembered the night of the circus, when Kieran had disappeared and then returned with his face looking flushed, and Philip had inquired as to whether he "felt better."

"My dear cousin—you are too easily led astray. Those are only myths, I assure you. Don't you think that *I* of all people should know?"

He slowly turned and walked over to where my letters to Valerie lay on the floor and stooped to pick them up. He waved them at me. "You're not sure how you feel about me, Selena? On the contrary, I think you do. But that is not something you will admit to your friend Valerie, or to me, or Philip…or even to yourself."

"No!" I cried, and ran from the room. The only thing I could think of was that I had to escape, that things were much worse than I had thought, and that I couldn't afford to let the feelings beginning to bloom inside me develop any further. I ran out the front gate, out of the castle, over the drawbridge, and down the rutted road that led to Castle Cormoran. The sky was overcast with threatening rainclouds, which served only to make the landscape seem even more forbidding, as if it were trying to tell me that there would be no escape.

From behind me, I heard a snarling sound, and the pounding of feet. Casting a quick glance back over my shoulder, I saw the big black dog, Mephistopheles, gaining on me, jaws snapping and eyes rolling as if he were mad. A lone tree, not very tall, and with its lowest branches perhaps four feet from the ground, stood several paces to the north. I turned and raced for it, Mephistopheles snapping at my heels. Sheer terror made me put forth a tremendous burst of speed, and even though I had never been very good at either gymnastics or acrobatics, I scrambled up that tree as fast as my arms and feet would allow.

No sooner had I gotten into the tree and the second of my feet had just left a low branch on my way up, but the dog was jumping at the tree trunk, snapping his jaws. I couldn't imagine why he had been chasing me so ferociously and now seemed as though he were hoping to shake me out of the tree and eat me alive. Something told me that this was no ordinary dog—his eyes seemed to be fairly rolling in his head, and he was foaming at the mouth. I climbed higher into the tree, and as I put my foot upon a branch, I heard a sickening crack. Just as the branch gave way, sending me crashing through the branches below, I thought I heard Kieran's voice from far away, calling off the dog. I fell to the ground, and everything turned black.

***

I approached my bed and drew back the drapes, to find Kieran sprawled across its middle on his back, propped up on his elbows and with one knee drawn up. He was shirtless, and his long black hair tumbled down wildly over his bare shoulders and chest. I could do nothing but stand and stare at him as his smoldering eyes cast their spell on me once again.

"I've been waiting for you," he said in that huskily seductive voice. "Come and kiss me."

Slowly I climbed on top of him, pushing him down into the mattress as I kissed his lips and caressed the smoothness of his face, the softness of his hair. "Make love to me, Selena," he whispered, "as I drive you mad with desire."

"Kieran," I said softly, "you've already driven me mad."

"Forget Philip," Kieran said. "You know I'm the only one that you want."

"Yes," I whispered, my voice barely audible, even to my own ears, "I know."

"You don't love him, Selena. You love only me."

"Yes, Kieran. Only you. I have always loved only you."

Kieran's fingertips gently stroked my cheek, then pulled my face down for me to kiss him again. After kissing me slowly, sensuously, with a kiss that seemed to swallow my very soul, he turned his head and sank his teeth into my neck.

"*Kieran!*" I shrieked, my eyes flying open. I struggled to get up, but a gentle hand pushed me back against the pillows.

"Rest easy, luv," Eugenia said. "You've had quite a nasty fall."

I could only stare at Eugenia in bewilderment. Had I been dreaming? How could it have seemed so real? I had never had such disturbingly realistic dreams before coming to Castle Cormoran, and it scared me.

"Kieran's gone to bed," Eugenia went on. "He was at your bedside all night, worried sick. I had to insist that he go on to bed."

"You mean you sent him back to his coffin at the crack of dawn," I said dryly.

Eugenia looked shocked. "Whatever are you babbling about, my dear? You must have really bumped your head when you fell out of that tree."

"How did I get back here?"

"Kieran brought you, of course. If he hadn't been there, heaven only knows what might have happened. He carried you back to your chamber himself. I'm sure Philip would have done the same, had he been there," she added quickly. "He tried to come in and keep watch over you, but Kieran wouldn't allow it."

A light rap sounded at the door, and Eugenia went to answer it. I propped myself up in bed and saw Derek standing in the doorway, frantically signing with his hands. Eugenia came back to my bed as I quickly lay back down.

"I'm afraid I must go. Just stay in bed and get some rest, luv. I'll leave your door open so you can call for Philip or Kieran if you need anything. I'd recommend that you not try to get up, dear. A head injury is not to be taken lightly." With that, she left the room.

I watched Eugenia's departure with mixed feelings. I wanted so much to trust her, but didn't know whether I dared. Could she really be so blissfully unaware of Kieran's true nature, or was she trying to protect him? Had she anything to do with my novels and the newspaper clippings in the sideboard? Or was that merely Kieran's doing? I couldn't deny the fact that one of the items in the stack was the letter I had written Eugenia.

I wondered whether I could trust Philip, either. I remembered only too well the conversation I had overheard between the two men, and wondered whether Philip's sensitivity was genuine. Perhaps he and Eugenia were both sheltering Kieran's nasty secret. Why not?—they were so vocal about being "family." I wasn't sure how I fit into all this, but I decided I did not want to be included in a family that was sheltering a vampire. What was worse, I feared that Kieran was going to try to put a spell on me, to sap my will, and I had to get out of there before Philip and Eugenia let him do it. Swinging my legs over the side of the bed, I got up and dressed as quickly as I could, considering I was still somewhat dizzy. I stuffed my camera and a change of underwear into my purse and peered out into the hall. There was no sign of anyone about. I ran on tiptoe down the hallway and down the steps that spiraled down one of the towers. I crept down the downstairs hall of the gatehouse and out the front gate, where I broke into a mad run.

I was perhaps a hundred yards from the castle's front gate when I heard hoofbeats behind me. Terrified, I threw a glance over my shoulder and saw Ellen, mounted on Ianthe, galloping across the bridge. I tried to put forth a fresh burst of speed, to reach the trees ahead of me, where I might perhaps find a place to hide. I knew there was no way I was going to outrun that horse.

Since it was only early spring, the vegetation in the woods was not as dense as I'm sure it must be in the summer, and suitable hiding places were scarce. I picked the densest bush I could find and crawled under it, where I huddled with my knees drawn up and branches scraping my head and arms. I sat very still, scarcely daring to breathe, but my heart was pounding with such force that I thought surely it must be audible.

I saw Ianthe coming down the path, picking her way slowly and carefully now. As she drew closer, I saw Ellen peering into the trees, turning her head from side to side. I crouched, frozen, under the bush, my knees weak and my heart thumping painfully against my ribs. My lungs felt as though they were on fire from my marathon sprint, and my throat and sinuses burned.

Ellen and Ianthe finally passed me, and I inwardly breathed a sigh of relief. I stayed under the bush for what must have been close to half an hour, afraid to come out lest they doubled back. But I saw dark clouds rolling in overhead again, so I crept out from my hiding place, my legs now cramped, and headed in the direction of Wittcombe.

The rain was just starting as I reached the outskirts of town, and I hurried to take shelter at a post office.

"Excuse me," I said to the man behind the counter. "Is there somewhere around here where I could place an overseas call?"

The man shook his head. "Sorry, mum."

"How about a telegraph? A wire?"

The man shook his head again. "Sorry, mum."

I was growing frustrated. "Look, I'm in trouble. I need to contact someone in the United States. It's an emergency!"

"Why don't you send them a letter?"

"That would *take* too damn long! Please, is there a way I can get from here to Leeds—to *anywhere* where I can get a train to London?"

"Might be able to round something up. Where you staying, mum?"

"Well, I *was* staying at Castle Cormoran—"

A dead silence settled over the post office. The other three or four customers standing around were all giving me the same suspicious, repulsed stare as the postal worker.

"Maybe you'd better be taking your business elsewhere, mum," the postal worker said coldly.

"Why? What's wrong?"

"We don't serve anyone from that place."

"I don't *live* there. I'm visiting from the United States—"

"I'm aware of that, mum, but anyone associated with that place is not welcome here. Now, I'm going to have to ask you to leave."

"You don't understand! I'm in trouble! I need help!"

"Aye, you'll be needing help, indeed," a bystander agreed, "coming from that cursed place!"

"What—?" I began, but another woman cut me off.

"Perhaps you wouldn't mind telling me what happened to my daughter?" she demanded. "Went to sign on there as a cook and never came back."

"I have no idea," I said lamely.

"That cursed *beast* took her, that's what! Don't be acting like you don't *know* what goes on there! You're a de Montfort, *too*, aren't you?"

I turned then and fled the post office, out into the rain. Bitter tears stung my cheeks. I had to find someone to help me. I had to get away, to put as much distance between myself and Castle Cormoran as possible.

As I darted across the street, eager to get out of the rain, a long black car screeched to a halt, narrowly missing hitting me. I took one glance at it and my heart seemed to turn to ice. I saw Derek jump out of the car, and I took off in the opposite direction. Being mute, he obviously couldn't shout at me to stop; but somehow I felt as though he had. I knew he was running after me, gaining on me, and suddenly I felt him grab my arm and yank me backwards.

"Let me go!" I screamed, trying desperately, and in vain, to fight him off. He just shook his head stubbornly as he dragged me back to the car and roughly shoved me into the back seat.

The rain and the thunderclouds accompanied us back to the castle, seeming to foretell my doom. Word had obviously gotten out about my escape—or perhaps I should say, my *attempted* escape—and the entire household would know about it when I got back. I was developing a horrible feeling in the pit of my stomach, for I knew I had just sentenced myself to a prison term. After I had almost gotten away, Kieran was *certain* to keep me under close surveillance now.

Kieran stood in the front doorway of the gatehouse as Derek stopped the car out front and led me back to the castle. Kieran's arms were folded over his chest, and a dark storm seemed to be brewing from within him, a storm far worse than the one rolling in from above us. Seeing him looking so angry, so fierce, seemed to me both terrifying and arousing at once. Just as Kieran had apparently enjoyed it when I had called him "a fucking animal," so, for some reason, I found the anticipation of an explosion from him strangely thrilling. It dawned on me at that moment that I found him incredibly sexy when he was angry—his eyes seemed to shoot off sparks, his jaw tightened, and his whole body seemed electrically charged.

"What do you mean by trying to run away?" Kieran demanded.

"What do *you* mean by trying to keep me here?" I retorted. It occurred to me then that I actually derived pleasure from challenging him. Perhaps I wanted to see how far I could push him before he snapped.

Kieran's voice dropped. "You like to play hard to get, don't you? You certainly can tease—but are you willing to follow through?"

"Look who's talking about being a tease. You've been tossing sexual innuendoes at me ever since I got here—not to mention the looks you're always giving me."

"I haven't offered you anything which you cannot have. Yet still you run away from me, even after repeatedly crying out my name in the middle of the night. And I know what you are dreaming when you call my name. I know all your dreams, Selena, all your thoughts. I know just how you feel about me, even if *you* don't."

I glared at him and tried to brush past, but he grasped my upper arm and held me fast.

"'Tis difficult for you to admit, is it not?" Kieran said, his voice scarcely more than a husky whisper. "I've put you in touch with your darker feelings...lust...anger...fear...feelings that you try so hard to bury, thinking that if you ignore them, they will go away. But they don't go away, Selena. They fester inside you; they eat you alive. Your parents raised you to be a good little Catholic girl, with a guilty conscience and a fear of the flesh. But you and I are more alike than you think. We share the same blood, and the same evil desires. Search your soul, cousin—you know it's true." He released my arm. "You can never escape me, Selena. I will haunt you till your dying day. I'm a part of you, dear cousin." He leant close to my ear. "You've drunk my blood."

With a strangled cry, I covered my mouth with one hand and fled inside the gatehouse.

Chapter Nine

The Secret

I ran all the way up the stairs to my bedchamber, where I slammed and bolted the door and crumpled into a pitiful little heap on the floor beside it. I covered my face with my hands, unable to fathom the horror that overwhelmed me. Drunk his blood! He had to be lying! I had never done such a thing! But even as I tried to convince myself, I knew it was in vain. It came back to me then—the night when he had shared his wine with me, and I had complained that it tasted funny. Now I understood—he had mixed some of his blood in it, knowing he would be able to persuade me to drink it. Indeed, he knew me only too well—knew he would have a hard time convincing me to drink his blood from his body, but he had only to mix it in some red wine, in a sort of Unholy Communion, and I would drink it right down. So he wasn't lying, or exaggerating, when he said I shared his blood. He had gotten inside me, waging a war with my soul. He infiltrated my dreams, directing my passion away from Philip and toward himself. How could this be? What was happening to me?

Slowly, I opened the door and peered out into the hall. I had to find Philip and try to find out what was going on. Philip was my last hope. If I couldn't trust him, then I truly was on my own.

I crept down the hall and rapped softly on Philip's door. He answered it and seemed surprised at my appearance.

"Selena! Whatever is wrong?"

"Philip, you've got to help me!"

Philip ushered me into his bedchamber and closed the door. He led me over to his bed and had me sit down. "Tell me," he said gently.

"Why didn't you tell me about Kieran?" I demanded, afraid I was about to cry.

Philip stroked my hair. "I told you I would protect you, my dearest cousin."

"Why didn't you *tell* me?" I repeated.

Philip looked distraught. "I didn't think you would believe me."

"Why did you let me come here? Surely you knew what would happen!"

"I didn't—"

"What about all those clippings about me that were in Kieran's sideboard?" I blurted out. "And my books? Why did everyone act like they didn't know I was a writer?"

"I never saw any books. I saw only your birth certificate and your photograph. Eugenia wanted to bring you here to reunite the family. Yes, I knew about Kieran—I have always known about Kieran—and I should have stepped in, I know, I should have told you not to come. But I let my own selfishness get in the way. I did not intervene because I wanted you to come. I thought I could protect you from Kieran. 'Tis my own folly and selfishness that has brought this upon you, my love. I cannot even bring myself to ask for your forgiveness." He held me in his arms and kissed me. "Never fear," he whispered. "'Tis not too late."

And since it was too painful to confront my dreadful reality, I let Philip convince me.

***

I scarcely slept that night, for fear of Kieran's creeping into my room when I was asleep. I bolted the door and tightly latched the window, but that was not enough to make me feel safe. I lay wide awake in bed, thinking of garlic and crosses and holy water and wondering whether they actually had any effect. If Kieran could be up and about during the day, eat solid food, and drink wine, then how many of the other commonly-held ideas about vampires were also myths? I hadn't noticed any fangs on him, either, nor had I noticed his having bad breath or long fingernails. One thing about him that *had* struck me as peculiar was that no matter what time of the day or night, he never seemed to have even a hint of a five o'clock shadow.

Finally, overcome by exhaustion, I fell into a fitful sleep. I saw myself walking into a chapel. Even though I had never seen it before, somehow I knew that it must have been the chapel there at Cormoran. A figure dressed all in black, with long black hair, stood at the altar with his back to me. As I drew closer, he turned around and fixed me with his dark stare. He held a golden chalice in his smooth, fair-skinned hands. The corners of his mouth lifted slightly, in the vaguest hint of a smile. He offered me the chalice, which I slowly took from his hands. I looked down into the cup, expecting to see red wine; but instead, the contents were a deep red, and much thicker than wine.

"Drink my blood," Kieran whispered in my ear. "Drink it, Selena." I paused, staring down at the blood-filled chalice. "Drink it, and you may have my body as well."

I awoke with a start. I was certain I'd heard something at the window, but the drapes around my bed obscured my view. I scrambled out of bed to find Kieran fastening the window latch.

"What are you doing?" I demanded, my heart in my throat. "How did you get in here?"

Kieran turned slowly and gave me his smirky smile. "You really should be more careful about latching the window, cousin," he said. "You never know *what* might come in."

"I *did* latch the window," I said, as the sick crawling in the pit of my stomach developed fingers that began to claw at my insides. "What are you trying to do to me?" I demanded, with more bravado than I felt. "Are you trying to drive me crazy? Is that it? You've been getting bored these past few hundred years, so you've got nothing better to do than drive me out of my fucking mind?"

"Is that what I'm doing?" A wicked little smile played about the corners of his mouth. "Driving you *mad*?"

My face flamed as he reminded me of the dream I had had only that morning—or sometime earlier in the day—before I'd regained consciousness after my fall from the tree. *"I know all your dreams, Selena, all your thoughts,"* he had said. *"I know just how you feel about me, even if you don't."*

"Am I truly driving you mad," Kieran asked, his voice low, "or are you perhaps doing it to yourself? Perhaps 'tis only how you feel about me that drives you mad."

"What is that supposed to mean?" I choked.

"I think you know *exactly* what it means." He looked terribly smug as he headed for the door.

"Why are you *doing* this to me?" I screamed at his back as he left the room.

"M'lady," Kieran said as he closed the door, "you do it to yourself."

I sank down to the floor, burying my face in my hands and crying. Was this a punishment for my wavering faith? Had I brought it upon myself? I wasn't sure of anything anymore. And that was perhaps the most frightening thing of all.

***

I was determined to get up early the next morning and locate the most recent portion of the family tree. I wanted to see whether perhaps it might divulge a clue as to where I fit into all this madness. I was up at the crack of dawn, rummaging through the shelves in the library, thinking that maybe I might find it stuffed behind a book, as I had the last one. But of course whoever had hidden it was much too clever to use the same trick twice, I discovered. After nearly fruitless searching, I found a wadded-up piece of paper jammed inside a silver cigarette box. My heart pounded as I smoothed the paper out on top of the library desk. I looked at the bottom of the page. At the far right was my name. Above it were the names of my parents—Kathryn Ramsey and Anthony D'Agostino. I carefully scanned the rest of the names. Kieran had been right—there were no more Kieran Ramseys to be found…so obviously, he *had* to be the Kieran Ramsey born in 1575. I shuddered. But then, an even more disturbing fact presented itself.

No Philip de Montforts had been born into the family in over 150 years.

I looked along the bottom of the chart again. I seemed to be the sole survivor. No one had been born into the de Montfort portion of the family since 1871. That meant Philip wasn't accounted for—and neither was Eugenia.

I sat staring numbly at the chart, as though perhaps if I focused on it long enough, Philip's and Eugenia's—and maybe even Kieran's—names might appear. But of course I knew it was no use. I got up on shaking legs and left the library, lurching across the inner ward to the outside door which I surmised must open into the chapel. I turned the handle and jiggled it violently, then threw my weight against it. I knew that something lay behind that door that the other family members did not want me to see, and that made me all the more determined to find out what it was. Perhaps it was a crypt—but I did not want to ponder how many coffins I might find there.

The door suddenly gave way, swinging open wide as though to usher me inside. I stepped into the chapel and gagged on the putrid stench that assaulted my nostrils. The first rays of early morning shone through the stained glass windows, still brilliant after six centuries. I found myself staring at a window that depicted the Archangel Michael, with long, amber-colored hair and dressed in the armor of a Crusader, trodding upon a fearsome black devil and piercing him with his broadsword. I was eerily reminded of the portrait of the young knight in the Great Hall, who looked so like Philip and had so vividly called St. Michael to mind. I tore my eyes away from the window and looked at the altar. Even though I knew I could never have seen it before, it looked familiar. Then I remembered: I had seen it in my dream, when Kieran had handed me the chalice full of his blood. I looked at the nave, surprised to see that there were no pews. Instead, there seemed to be heaps of dirt and rubbish. I took a step further into the chapel, and my foot struck something. I looked down to see what it was. It was a human skull.

I slapped a hand over my mouth to keep from screaming. Quickly, I looked about the nave, realizing in horror that the heaps of what appeared at first glance to be rubbish were actually the remains of decomposing corpses. No wonder there was such an unbearable stench…no wonder they kept the door locked. I felt the bile rising in my throat, threatening to choke me. I turned to go back out the way I had come, but I found the door shut. No amount of pushing and struggling could convince it to open.

The thought of being locked up in a chapel full of human remains was almost more than I could bear. I ran to the other door, which opened from the chapel to the Great Hall, but it too was locked. I prowled around the periphery of the chapel, hoping to find some other exit. I found a loose stone in the floor, and when I removed it, I found part of a stair. I moved three stones around it and saw the beginning of a stairway leading down into the bowels of the earth—or so it seemed. Slowly, I descended the stairs and made my way down a dark passageway. I've always had a sort of phobia about tunnels, particularly subterranean ones, and I could not see very well besides, so to say that I was feeling intense fear would be an understatement. I emerged into a rather large chamber, in which someone had left a couple of torches burning which cast eerie shadows on the walls. I realized that I was in the castle catacombs, and that the large stone monuments around me were actually tombs. My eye fell upon one which had its stone lid pushed aside, revealing the wooden coffin lid beneath. I read the inscription on the coffin's stone side:

Kieran Ramsey
November 12, 1575—April 5, 1604

November 12. That was *my* birthday. And Kieran had been twenty-eight when he died. That was exactly how old I was now.

I turned and fled back down the passageway, up the stairs, and into the chapel. Beating on the door, I screamed to be let out. I was nearly ready to collapse in frustration and exhaustion when the door was slowly opened to reveal Derek's sour face. A look of surprise settled on his features as his eye fell upon me, but I had no time for pleasantries or explanations. I roughly brushed past him and ran all the way to my chamber, where I stayed the rest of the day, my door bolted and my soul in a state of mortal fear.

***

I did not wish to leave my room, even when Derek came to summon me that evening. I had spent the better part of the day pacing the floor, too tense and fidgety to sit still. Now I was certain that I could trust no one in this household, not even the servants, who were too frightened of, and subservient to, their employers to risk their wrath by helping me. Were the corpses in the chapel the remains of Kieran's victims—perhaps the hapless servants who had angered him in the past? Perhaps he had even been the blue mist that night in the inner ward, and the black cat in my bed. I recoiled at the horrific images that paraded across my mind, having to do with corpses, blood, raw meat. I had felt, upon our first meeting, that Kieran was a man of many secrets and not to be trusted; but I hadn't thought him capable of murdering people and drinking their blood. I put my hands to my temples, as though to squeeze from my mind the memories of Kieran's holding me close as he taught me how to waltz, of the night he had been in my bed with his hand up under my nightgown. I felt certain now that he had lied about not having been there—I *knew* it wasn't a dream. I had never been so electrified by a man's touch. Not even Philip's.

Both Philip and Kieran had knocked at my door during the late afternoon, and I had emphatically told both of them to get lost. Derek came later and was quite adamant about my coming down to dinner, so reluctantly I followed him downstairs.

I took dinner alone that evening. Jane's eyes were downcast as she set my meal before me and then quickly scampered away. I ate little and without enthusiasm and then left the dining hall to return to my chamber. It was raining out, so I decided not to take the shortcut through the inner ward, instead going down the long, cavernous hallway back to the gatehouse. From around the bend a figure came striding purposefully in my direction. Even in the dimly lit hallway, it took only a split-second for my brain to register his dark hair, and I turned and ran the other way.

"Selena!" I heard him shout, his voice bouncing off the stone walls. I had gotten nearly to the Great Hall before he caught me, grabbing my arm and spinning me around to face him.

"Let go," I choked.

"You can't keep running away, cousin," Kieran said. "Soon you'll have to face the truth."

"I already know the truth."

"I don't think you know all of it...or at least, you won't admit it to yourself." He tightened his grip on my arm. "You found the rest of the family tree."

It seemed useless to lie. "Yes," I said.

"So you know about Philip."

"I know he's not like you."

"Will you listen to me?" Kieran hissed. "Stay away from him. Don't listen to him. You have to stop this. *Now.*"

I managed to jerk my arm free and gave him the evil eye. "Why don't you and Philip take your petty jealousies somewhere else?"

"Do you want to know *why* you were lured here?"

"So you admit it?"

"It wasn't my idea. Eugenia has been trying to find the surviving family members for years. She's dying, you know."

"No, I didn't know that. She doesn't look sick."

"Well, she is. Very sick. And since you're the only other woman left in the family, Eugenia and Philip thought it imperative to bring you here."

"For what?"

"You're to have Philip's child."

"*What?* What are you talking about?"

"You're family. You have the de Montfort blood in your veins as well."

I'd heard of royalty and aristocracy marrying distant (or sometimes not-so-distant) relations to keep their bloodlines "pure," but this was ridiculous.

"You *do* know about Philip," Kieran said, cocking an eyebrow at me.

My heart began to pound as I recalled not finding his name on the family tree, and then I remembered Kieran's nicking him with his blade—only a few hours later, Philip hadn't even a scratch. "What about him?" I asked slowly, my mouth very dry.

"Come—I wish to show you something," Kieran said, leading the way to the Great Hall. I reluctantly followed, and Kieran stopped in front of the portrait of the young knight who looked so much like Philip.

"My portrait was relegated to a little-used parlor, whilst Philip's has been allowed to hang all these centuries in a place of honor," Kieran said. "And I suppose you realize he was also the model for the window in the chapel depicting St. Michael. But let me assure you, m'lady—our fair cousin is neither a saint nor an angel."

"Neither are you," I said.

"True," Kieran said, inclining his head ever so slightly, "but I never tried to pass myself off as one, either."

What Kieran was trying to tell me seemed so outrageous, I couldn't possibly believe it. "If Philip *were* a vampire, he wouldn't be able to *have* children," I said.

"Not true. You've read too much popular fiction. Selena, my dear, you of all people should know—you can't believe everything you read."

"Are they intending to keep me a prisoner here?"

"If you left, you might tell others about us."

"Are you crazy? No one would believe me." My mind was racing. "What happens to me after I bear his children?"

"You either stay here—or he will kill you."

"Philip would never do that!" I exclaimed. I couldn't imagine Philip's killing anyone—least of all me—unless it had all been an act.

"I'm afraid I know Philip a lot better than *you* do, dear cousin. Though, granted, not as *physically* well." Kieran fixed me with that look he was always giving me. "He was already over three hundred years old when I was born. I've known him a long time. I don't think he's changed recently."

"Why should I believe *you*? How do I know *you're* not the one at the center of all this, rather than Philip?"

Kieran's jaw tightened. "Because I'm the family bastard. Philip is the only one whose blood is pure."

"And you expect me to believe you have nothing to do with any of this? That you're innocent?"

"I never said I was 'innocent.' But I've told you the truth. The whole scheme is Philip and Eugenia's invention."

"Then why did you have all that stuff about me—and my books—in your sideboard? And how—why—did you get a copy of my birth certificate?"

"You certainly like to pry, don't you? Incidentally, that is not 'my' sideboard. True, I have a few things stashed in there, but 'twas Eugenia who amassed that rather impressive collection. She journeyed to the

States a few months ago, after she discovered you. She wanted to be certain you were the genuine article—and she wanted some proof that you were one of ours. That is why she obtained several photographs of you, as well as examples of your talent. I've read the two books she brought back, though I understand you've written quite a few more. You truly are a very intelligent, talented woman, Selena. I'm looking forward to reading the rest of your novels."

I wasn't in the mood for compliments. "Philip said he was sterile," I said, trying to get him back on track.

"Philip was lying to you, m'lady."

"What is to be done with the children?"

"They remain here, of course. Their existence is meant to ensure the preservation of the family."

"Why now? Why didn't Philip do this a long time ago?"

"It wasn't until the twentieth century that the family began to die out. And you're mistaken. Philip does have a child. A daughter."

"Where is she? Is she dead?"

"Not yet." Kieran smiled indulgently. "You've already met her."

I reeled with the implication of what he was saying. "*Eugenia?*"

Kieran inclined his head in that mocking way. "Eugenia."

"Rather than being his mother, she's his *daughter*? Why didn't *she* have children?"

"She can't. She's barren. Did you know…" Kieran settled back against the wall and folded his arms. "…her mother was a practitioner of the black arts?"

"You're pulling my leg."

Kieran shook his head. "After giving birth to Eugenia, seeing what their union had produced, she threw herself from her bedroom window."

Insight dawned upon me. "She's the woman with the lantern!"

Kieran nodded.

"And Ellen scrubbing the cobblestones—the bloodstain—that was the spot where she landed? It keeps coming back because that's the spot where she landed! And Ellen keeps scrubbing it away, but it comes back…You gave me *her* room?"

"You're babbling, m'lady." Kieran looked thoughtful. "That was Philip's mistake—choosing a woman like that, when he should have chosen an ordinary mortal." He smiled wickedly. "Someone like you…except perhaps that you are not so ordinary yourself."

"So how did Philip become a vampire?"

"He was on his way home from the Crusades—the Fifth Crusade, to be exact—and their ship made a stop on the Greek island of Santorini, I suppose for supplies or whatever. Philip apparently made quite an impression on the local ladies—he always wore his hair unfashionably long, and with his pretty-boy looks and impeccable manners, he turned a few heads. He caught the fancy of a very beautiful—so I'm told—young woman who lured him to her house one night whilst the others were asleep. She drank his blood, fed him some of hers, and then killed him. He made the rest of the journey home in a wooden box." Kieran paused for a moment, a brief hint of a smile playing about the corners of his mouth. "You can imagine the surprise of the other family members when he was spied walking round the grounds at night, and the villagers were being terrorized by a blood drinker who made his presence felt but was never identified. Philip became the nasty little family secret, which they tried in vain to confine to the family crypt for the next three hundred years or so. Then I was born."

"How did *you* become one, then?"

"That was Philip's doing, of course. We were quite distant cousins, and despite the fact that I was illegitimate, he was quite jealous of me once I began growing up. My mother saw to it that I was well-versed in all the gentlemanly pursuits—riding, duelling, hunting, music—and even persuaded my father to send me to Oxford, where I was at the top of my class. Even though I had no claim to a title or the family estate, I was the perfect modern gentleman of the time, and Philip was eaten up with jealousy. Here I could go anywhere, anytime, do whatever I wanted; I was free to court ladies and pursue a life of gentlemanly leisure, whilst Philip was banished to the family crypt, unable to indulge in all the creature comforts. What's more, unlike most of the family, I was never afraid of him. He wanted to bring me down to his level, I suppose, to make me experience the hell he had to endure. He set upon me one night whilst I slumbered in my bed, ripping my neck to shreds and draining my blood. My brother Ferdinand—from whom you are descended—found me the next morning, dead."

"And you've been rivals ever since."

"Aye. We've always fought bitterly, but at the core of it all—we're still family."

"So I'm expected to think of you as a victim?"

"I don't think of myself as a victim…more like a man who makes the most of the bad situations, as well as opportunities."

"And what do *you* want out of me?"

"What makes you think I want something?"

"You wouldn't act like you were trying to save me from Philip if you didn't want something yourself."

"You don't believe I am merely trying to protect you?"

"You?—no. Not really. I've had the feeling you had something up your sleeve ever since I got here."

Kieran stepped close to me and lightly ran his fingertips down my arm. "I can give you that which you crave," he said near my ear, his voice very low.

My heart pounded painfully. I didn't know whether it was fear, or an emotion even more frightening. I wasn't going to get mixed up with him, I told myself. I wasn't.

"Which is—?" I squeaked.

Kieran's lips were nearly touching my ear. "Immortality."

I felt strangely hot and cold, both at once. "Why me?" I whispered as Kieran touched my hair.

"You are the lover, the bride I never had. Even your name concurs...Selena, the moon, lighting up the darkness of my night. We're two sides of the same coin, two halves of one soul. My blood is in your veins...and your blood is in mine." He moved even closer, his body touching mine and sending shockwaves through me. "I've grown quite fond of you, my dear Selena," he said, his voice growing huskier still. "I knew you wanted me the night we met. I know what you feel even before you do. You're burning me alive in the fire of your lust, roasting me as surely as if you were turning me upon a spit. You knew that wasn't Philip in your bed that night. You invited me into your dreams; you opened wide your soul to me, begging me to come in and take possession of it. Didn't you?"

I found I had no voice with which to answer him.

"You've been deceiving yourself, my lady—but you can't deceive me. No other man will ever know your heart and soul the way that I do. You came here looking for your heritage...this is it, Selena. Your past and your future are staring into your eyes."

I tried to swallow, but my throat felt strangely constricted.

"'Tis what you've always wanted, is it not—immortality? You thought you could achieve it with your writing, but I am offering it to you in truth...in the flesh. Can the printed page give eternal life to your words the way that I can to your body, your mind?

"Think of all the books you could write. Think how rich you could become. You'd never grow old. You'd never die. You'd never have a worry again. To hell with Philip and Eugenia. 'Tis only you and I that matter. You and I are meant to be together, Selena. 'Twas your destiny to come here and to find me. 'Tis our blood that unites us."

I finally found my voice. "And I suppose blood means a lot to you," I whispered, "being what you are."

"I need it to survive. So do you understand when I say you are my blood?"

Kieran ran his hand down the side of my face, over my cheek, turning my face to kiss my lips. I felt as though I were drowning, unable to resist and not really wanting to. Every nerve-ending in my body felt as though it were on fire as Kieran's other arm slithered around my waist and pulled me tight against him. It would have been so easy to give in, to have let him sweep me up into his arms and whisk me off to his bed, to lose myself in his kiss, his long black hair, his smoldering eyes. But I've always been something of a fighter, and when Kieran's lips lost touch with mine for the briefest of moments, I twisted free of his grasp and ran, gasping, for the door, yanking it open and running like hell.

"*Selena!*" I heard his voice roaring after me, but I didn't dare look back. I knew then it wasn't fear that I felt.

It was something much worse.

Chapter Ten

The Blaze

I fled to my chamber and pulled my suitcases from under the bed, flinging them on top of the mattress and yanking them open. Then I flew over to the wardrobe and began tearing my clothes out and tossing them into my suitcases, with no regard for the wrinkles I was putting into everything. Panic fuelled my motions—panic that if I stayed so much as one day longer, I would *never* be able to leave. I wasn't certain which was more insidious: Kieran's security force—the mute servants and the vicious dog that he used to bring me back—or the spell he was putting on me, seducing me so that I wouldn't *want* to leave. I told myself I had to get out.

I opened my purse to make certain I still had my airline ticket but couldn't find it. Frenzied, I dug through my purse again, then emptied its contents onto the bed. Not only my airline ticket, but my passport, folding currency, and traveller's checks were also gone. Someone had left me exactly two pounds and 57 pence in change. I wasn't going to get very far on *that*, and without my passport, I couldn't even leave the country. I left the room, storming across the hall to Kieran's bedroom. The door was unlocked, so I let myself in. I couldn't believe he would stoop so low as to steal my personal possessions from my purse; but if he had them hidden in his room, I had every intention of taking them back. I no longer cared about propriety or discretion—I had to get the hell out of there.

Digging through the contents of Kieran's drawers, I came upon his diploma from Oxford, some frail-looking letters which I did not stop to read, and a very ancient-looking drawing that appeared to have been done by a child. It depicted three people riding horses. Two of them were small, so I figured they must have been children. The third figure was larger and had long black hair. I stood staring at the picture for a moment, my eyes beginning to blur a little. Kieran had never married or had any children, but this picture seemed to indicate that perhaps he had a couple of favorite nephews that he had taken riding. Obviously an excellent horseman, perhaps Kieran himself had even taught the boys to ride. At any rate, at least one of the boys remembered the activity fondly enough to commit it to paper. One of those boys might even have been one of my ancestors, since Kieran had said I was descended from his brother Ferdinand. A man who took the time to entertain his young nephews couldn't be *all* bad, surely; but that was a long time ago, when things were different. Angry at myself, I thrust the drawing aside and found myself staring into the drawer at a photograph of myself. Slowly I picked it up, wondering how it had gotten there. It must have been taken at least two years before. A horribly creepy feeling came over me, as if I were being watched, and I threw the photo back into the drawer and slammed it shut. I turned and fled the room.

I returned to my own chamber to find Kieran sitting in a side chair, tilted back on the chair's hind legs as his feet, legs crossed at the ankle, rested on top of the dresser. He looked up at my entrance, and my eye fell upon my notebook, which I had been keeping as a journal, in his hands.

"How dare you read that!" I cried, lunging for it. Kieran twisted and leapt from the chair in one long, graceful movement, jumping back out of my reach.

"'Tis a funny thing to hear coming from someone so fond of snooping," Kieran said glibly. "But then, you've always been full of contradictions, aye, m'lady? The good little Catholic girl with the dirty mind."

"I left the Catholic Church nearly ten years ago," I said irritably.

"Aye, but it haunts you still. That guilty conscience your parents planted in you will never give you rest."

"Just give me my journal," I said, reaching for it.

Kieran jerked his arm back, holding the journal behind his head, out of my reach. "How badly do you want it?"

"Cut it out."

"'Tis fascinating reading, dear cousin." Kieran smiled wickedly. "I was only getting to the best part. I'm flattered you've devoted the lion's share of it to me."

"Don't flatter yourself too much," I retorted, with more bravado than I felt.

Kieran slowly turned and strolled several steps away, taking the journal from behind his head and casting a critical eye upon it. Then, in one quick motion, he tossed it into the fireplace, into the crackling flames. I leapt forward, but it was already gone.

"What are you *doing*?" I cried. "How *dare* you—!"

Kieran came to stand close before me. "What have you written in that book that you do not carry here?" He placed his hand over my heart, which pounded wildly. "Or here?" he added, moving his hand to touch my forehead, as he gently kissed my temple. "You will never forget me, nor the magical things you are feeling. You will carry them with you always. I'm in your blood, Selena. I surge through your veins; I am inside you, making love to your soul."

"What have you done with my airline ticket?" I asked softly, my voice sounding old and tired. "And my passport? And my money?"

Kieran looked offended. "You think *I* took them?"

"Why shouldn't I? You're the one who so obviously wants to keep me here."

"Perhaps before you go round making accusations, you should talk to Eugenia."

"All right," I said, taking a deep breath. "Where is she?"

A wicked gleam shone from Kieran's eye as he said, "You shall probably find her in the chapel."

I left the room, making my way to the chapel. I found the door unlocked and opened it, stepping inside. "Eugenia?" I called. It was getting late in the evening, and no light shone through the massive stained glass windows. Several sconces around the walls were lit, casting a dim glow on the chapel's interior. As my eyes adjusted to the dimness, my gaze fell upon a figure crouched upon the floor. I realized, to my horror, that it was Eugenia.

The scene before me was so dreadful, so surreal, and yet, became etched so permanently upon my mind. Eugenia, usually the picture of civilized, upper-class British matriarchy, was hunched over a limp body. Her hair and clothes were a mess, her eyes seemed to be those of a demon, and her mouth and chin were smeared with blood. I glanced at the form in her arms and was further horrified to discover that it was Sissy, the cook who had "quit" just a few days before. Most of the flesh was gone from her upper arm, and it appeared that Eugenia was not drinking her blood in the manner of a vampire—Sissy had obviously already been dead for a few days, from the looks of her—but was in fact *eating her flesh.* My body became wracked with dry heaves, and I turned to flee, bumping into someone. I involuntarily screamed.

Philip put his arms out to stop me, and I looked at his face and saw a trace of red at one side of his mouth. There was also a red stain on the wrist of his right shirtsleeve, as though he had just been wiping blood from his mouth.

"Let me go!" I cried, struggling to get past him.

"Selena! Calm yourself!" he said.

"Calm myself? *Calm myself?* I'm alone in a castle with my supposed relatives who are all vampires and ghouls and ghosts, and you expect me to *calm* myself?! You lied to me, Philip, you no-good son-of-a-bitch!" I burst into tears.

"Lied to you?"

"Of course you lied! You lied about *everything*!" I broke free from his grasp and ran for the gatehouse. I had not even made it to the stairs when I ran into Kieran.

"I trust you found Eugenia, then?" he said.

I tried to pound his chest with my fists, but he grasped my arms and held me fast. I was nearly overcome with frustration and despair. "Why me?"

"If you hadn't seen it with your own eyes, you would never have believed me." Kieran led me back upstairs to my chamber, and I was too exhausted to resist. He deposited me on the bed and bolted the door. I sat staring at him morosely.

"This shouldn't happen to a dog," I said miserably.

Kieran turned and fixed me with his unfathomable gaze. "I tried to warn you."

"Like I should put my trust in a vampire."

"Better me than Philip and Eugenia."

I snorted. "Some choice."

Kieran shook his head. "My dear, dear cousin, you're a very intelligent woman, but you're no judge of character. You get taken in much too easily by those you should not trust, and are too suspicious of those you should."

"Oh, now you're going to point out all my faults to me? Okay, fine. But let's not forget some of *yours*. Take lying, for example."

"I've told you only two lies, m'lady."

"I don't think you can count, then."

"I count very well. The first was when I said I hadn't been in your bed, and the second was when I said that I became a perfect beast when I drank, when in fact drinking has nothing to do with it. I am *always* a beast."

"How about..." My voice trailed off as I realized that I *couldn't* think of any other lies he'd told.

"Please don't confuse me with Philip, m'lady," Kieran said. "I'm afraid our fair cousin has many more lies to his credit—or perhaps his *dis*credit—than I. And I'm sorry I laughed at you about the blue mist. 'Tis true I *didn't* see it, but I'm sure 'twas Philip, popping over to the servants' quarters for a bite."

"Please spare me the dreadful puns."

"Philip was also the black cat in your bed. So you see, m'lady, he invaded your privacy before I did."

"He told me Sissy quit, but she's...she's dead..."

"Aye, and I'm sure Philip blamed that on me as well, did he not?"

"He did say something about thinking perhaps you'd scared her off."

Kieran snorted. "I'm afraid I had nothing to do with Sissy's demise. Philip drank his fill of her, and now Eugenia shall polish her off."

"That's disgusting!"

"Aye, that it is, I suppose. Do you know where Eugenia vanishes to every other day or so? She has Derek keep abreast of all the recent burials in the vicinity and chauffeur her round for a good meal."

"Kieran, stop it!"

But Kieran was just warming to his subject. "I don't suppose Philip has told you what he does with the servant girls...or why Eugenia insists on having mute servants."

"So they won't squeal, I suppose."

"Aye, and if they don't come mute already, Eugenia sees to it personally that they are by the time they are hired. I don't suppose you've ever seen Ellen open her mouth?"

I slowly shook my head, dreading what I knew was coming.

"Then you won't have noticed that she has no tongue. You see, m'lady, you're not the first visitor since the rest of the family passed on. None of the others have left alive—in fact, they haven't left at all. You may still see their bones in the chapel. But you're the lucky one, dear cousin—you won't be allowed to leave, but with my protection, you will at least be allowed to stay alive."

"Stop it! I don't want to hear any more!"

"You can't run from the truth, m'lady. This is your family. You can't change who you are, Selena, or where you come from."

"At least *I'm* not a vampire or a ghoul."

"Do you think any of us *chose* what we are? Do you think that Eugenia has not wept to be a normal woman—like you—who could go out into the world, make friends, fall in love, bear children? Do you think Philip did not feel pain at being deprived a hero's welcome when he returned from the Crusades, to instead be regarded as an object of horror and embarrassment?" Kieran stepped closer to where I sat on the bed, looking down at me with his hypnotic eyes. "And what about *me*, Selena?" he asked, his voice dropping. "Have you no idea what I feel? How I savor our first meeting, m'lady. You found me intriguing and attractive, did you not? I mesmerized you. But that was before you discovered the truth, before you allowed your fear to take you prisoner. How I wish you would allow yourself to give yourself as willingly to me in your waking hours as you do in your dreams. For in your dreams you shall discover the truth of your feelings."

I was fighting for composure, biting back my pride as I said, "Please, Kieran, don't keep me here. I'll go mad. If you just let me go home, I promise I'll never tell anyone about you. Please just let me go, Kieran. Don't do this to me."

"Selena," he said, very seriously, "I cannot. 'Twould be as if I'd ripped my own heart from my chest. You are my heart, my lady, the blood that runs hot in my veins. To let you go—I would be driving a stake through my own heart."

I turned away from him, flinging myself to the far side of my bed, where I lay still, too numb to even cry.

***

I scarcely slept that night, kept awake by the terrified hammering of my heart. The only time I actually fell asleep was for but a short time, and then, not surprisingly, I again dreamt of Kieran. We were making love in a coffin lined in red satin, and surrounded by black roses. Kieran was on top of me, tenderly kissing my neck before sinking his teeth into it. He slurped my blood from my neck and then, pulling away, bit down hard on his own tongue, so that several drops of his blood squirted into my mouth.

"Now you cannot deny the bond that unites us," he whispered. "If ever you doubted that we were of one blood, surely you can no longer…Selena…my love."

I jerked awake. My neck throbbed, and I thought I tasted blood. I gently put my hand to my neck. It came away wet and red. *"Kieran!"* I screamed. But no one answered.

I sat up in bed, hugging my knees. My mind seemed to be racing in several directions at once, that doubled back on themselves and collided. I couldn't seem to unscramble the mess, to think logically. I knew I was no longer the same person I had been when I first came here: part of me had never felt so alive, and part of me had never felt so terrified. I knew I would never meet another man like Kieran, so adept at setting my soul on fire, so skillful at tempting me down such a dark, dangerous path. The idea of having a tireless, insatiable, immortal lover had its obvious appeal: Kieran had come through the past four centuries still a gorgeous twenty-eight; he would never grow old, never lose his looks; he would never slow down or suffer a mid-life crisis. I was unable to resist the lascivious thoughts that engulfed me, of tasting his lips, of undressing him, of savoring his body as he devoured me. I realized that I desperately wanted to be seduced by him, having him slowly drain away my will, so that I might completely, willingly surrender to him and not have to suffer guilt or exercise any measure of control. The problem was: Must I risk my soul in order to sample the pleasures of his body?

My parents had despaired when, at the tender age of eighteen, I had left the Roman Catholic Church, uncomfortable with many of its teachings, and declared myself an "agnostic." Still, something of the guilty Catholic conscience, with its endless taboos and fear of being cast into hell, still remained to torment me. Kieran had been right about that, I realized now; perhaps he had even gone through the same thing, in the days of his mortal youth. I thought about the things he had been telling me since my arrival at Cormoran, the fondness he had for pointing out that which I really didn't want to know. I began to wonder whether I might in fact be responsible for my own actions, my own feelings. Kieran could keep me prisoner there only as long as I wanted to be kept prisoner; he would visit me in my dreams only because I wanted him to be there. He *was* in my blood, feeding upon the dark, evil emotions within me. If I destroyed him, I could destroy the evil side of myself and thus set myself free. And I would set him free as well, for only when he could truly die, when his soul could at long last leave his body, would he find peace. All that would be left would be the soul of a musician and Oxford scholar, a young man devoted to his extended family because he had never had one of his own; a misfit with no title, no inheritance, save that which had been inflicted upon him by a jealous, Undead relative. Perhaps if his spirit were allowed to go across, he might be there waiting for me when my time came, to ease my fear of death. It was a very poignant, romantic thought, but it did little to disguise the awful horror of what I knew I must do.

***

At daybreak I was up and dressed. Into my shoulderbag I crammed my camera, my tapes, and a change of underwear. I knew I would have no time to return to my room and get anything, so I put on my black overcoat, clipped my Walkman to my belt, and slung my purse over my right shoulder so that the strap crossed my chest and the bag hung at my left hip. That way, I needn't worry about dropping it if I had to run. And I had a feeling I *would* have to run.

I quietly stole downstairs. No one seemed to be stirring, not even the servants. I made my way to the kitchen, where I searched all the cupboards until I found a large can of kerosene—used to light the household lamps—and a pack of matches. Then I quietly hurried to the small garden shed I had noticed by the stables. If I knew anything about vampires, it was that one dispatched them by driving a stake through their hearts. Needless to say, they were not going to have anything so handy as a spare stake lying around, waiting for someone to use it on them; so I looked around for something that would suffice in a pinch. My eye fell upon an old wooden stool, and I picked it up and smashed it against the floor, breaking off a leg. I then rummaged in my purse for the Swiss army knife that resided in the bottom depths. Suddenly, I was never so thankful as I was at that moment that my father had taught me, in my preteen years, to whittle, and had impressed upon me that there is no tool handier to have on one's person than a Swiss army knife. But never in my wildest dreams could I have envisioned that one day I would use that knife to whittle a stool leg into a stake for destroying a vampire.

I worked fast and furiously with my knife, and then broke another leg off the stool and repeated the task. The wood was old and worn and wasn't difficult to work with; I just hoped it would hold up to the task at hand. I then wondered: Does one have to use a certain type of wood for a stake? If my stool legs weren't sufficient, I was going to be in serious trouble.

Some further searching in the garden shed turned up a shovel, which I also appropriated. Staggering under the weight of my grim burden, I headed for the chapel.

The chapel door had been closed but not locked. I gently pushed it open and squeezed inside. The first dim shafts of sunlight filtered through the stained glass windows, but it was still too dark near the floor to distinguish the rotting corpses that lay there. I tried not to look at them as I gingerly picked my way across the chapel floor to the trap door leading to the crypt. I descended the stairs and took an unlit torch down from the wall and lit it with one of my matches. I struggled to drag my equipment all in one arm as I carried the torch in the other. When I reached the main chamber, I put down my things and used my torch to light a couple of other torches on the walls. With knees and hands shaking, I went in search of Philip's coffin. It did not seem to be near Kieran's, and I had to prowl deeper and deeper into the catacombs to find it. Finally, I found a coffin that said "Philip de Montfort." Luckily, the stone lid was pushed aside, but the wooden coffin lid was not, and it did not budge easily. I had to use my shovel as a lever, wedging the metal blade between the lid and the bottom part of the coffin and pushing down on the handle with all my strength. The lid shifted with a loud creak, and I used my hands to lift it and slide it back. Philip lay peacefully inside, looking so young, so innocent, his long, tawny hair cascading down his chest in soft waves, his long eyelashes resting gently against his smooth cheeks. I had to act quickly, before I changed my mind. I placed one of my stool leg stakes over the spot on his chest where I figured his heart was, took a deep breath, and came down on it as hard as I could with the head of the shovel.

I was not prepared for the dreadful result. Philip's eyes and mouth flew open; a horrible scream erupted from his lips and blood splurted from the wound. I gave the stake another blow with the shovel, driving it in deeper, and a great geyser of blood gushed up from around the stake. More blood splurted from his mouth and splattered my face and hair. I hastily gathered up my equipment and fled back the way I had come, stopping at Kieran's coffin.

I used the shovel to pry open Kieran's coffin, and when the lid slid off and clattered to the floor, I stood staring at the slumbering form that lay within. His eyes were closed, so for once I could look upon him without being held captive by his mysterious stare. He looked so peaceful, as though he were merely taking a refreshing nap. The lines of his face seemed to have relaxed, making him seem younger, more serene, with a quality to his face that bordered on sweetness. This surprised me, because I hadn't known Kieran was capable of looking like that. And even though I was obviously not held captive by his eyes at that moment, still I seemed to have fallen into a trance, unable to move. I was struck suddenly by how handsome he really was, how smooth and fair and flawless was his skin, how perfect the hands which were folded neatly over his chest. His long black hair was spread out beneath him, serving as a stunning backdrop for his beautifully striking face, and his lips looked soft and sweetly tempting. I felt a strong urge to bend over the coffin and kiss those lips; but I summoned every last ounce of my resolve, persuading myself to resist. I couldn't risk waking him, and if I gave in to him this time, I knew that I would never have my own strength of will again.

After the horrifying consequence of staking Philip, I was not about to put myself through that again; so, with tears beginning to blur my vision, I picked up the can of kerosene and gave Kieran's body a good dousing. I was shaking uncontrollably as I tried to strike a match. When finally I succeeded, I held the match aloft in one trembling hand and whispered, "*Goodnight, sweet prince—and flights of angels sing thee to thy rest.*"[1] With a sob, I flung the match into the coffin and jumped back.

Flames leapt up at once in a deadly conflagration, and a host of creatures began leaping out of the flames: snakes, lizards, toads, birds, rats, large spiders. I threw my arms over my head as a bird swooped at me, seemingly bent on getting entangled in my hair. Gathering my wits, I snatched up the shovel and began smashing the creatures over their heads as they tried to scurry away and threw their limp bodies into the flames. The birds were the hardest, because they usually took two whacks apiece: one to knock them out of the air, and another to smash

[1] William Shakespeare, *Hamlet*, Act V, Scene II

their skulls. It was an extremely distasteful task, made all the more difficult by the increasing speed with which they leapt from the coffin in all directions. I kept hitting them with the shovel, swinging it until my arms were so sore I could hardly hold them up. Finally, I flung the last snake into the flames, breathing a sigh of relief when nothing else jumped out at me. I dropped the shovel and picked up the kerosene can, pouring a trail of it across the floor as I made my way back to the stairs. I continued pouring as I backed up the stairs, and the kerosene ran out when I reached the chapel. I was fumbling with a match when a voice behind me demanded, "And just *what* do you think you're doing?"

I spun around with a gasp, to see Eugenia eyeing me malevolently. I held up the box of matches with a shaking hand. "Come any closer, and this whole place goes up in flames," I threatened.

"What have you done with Philip?"

I felt a slow, nefarious smile spread across my face. "Why don't you go see?"

Eugenia gave me another piercing look and fairly flew down the stairs. I scrambled to light a match and toss it down after her. The kerosene quickly ignited, and a long tongue of flame shot down the passageway. I dropped to my knees, grasping the stones that covered the stairwell and quickly sliding them back into place. Horrible screams echoed from below, and I cast about for something to seal the opening. I spied a heavy brass candlestand, which I dragged over and set upon the stones, and I ran for my life.

I raced for the stables. Mephistopheles was barking wildly. I opened Valiant's stall and shouted at him to get out. The horse bolted from the stable as if he understood. Next I opened Diogenes' stall. Kieran's fierce black stallion refused to budge, choosing to stand and eye me accusingly, as though he knew what I had done to his master. "Go!" I screamed at him. He didn't move. "The hell with you, then," I said, and ran to get Ianthe. I grabbed a raincoat that someone, probably Ellen, had left hanging on a peg on the wall, and threw it on over my bloody clothes. I quickly put Ianthe's harness on her and mounted her, not bothering with a saddle. I kicked her flanks and we raced out of the stables, out the castle gate to freedom.

I never found out what happened to the servants; I only hope they got out alive. I wasn't sure exactly where the servants' quarters were, and screaming at them to get out would have done no good. I hold on to the hope that they smelled the smoke or saw the flames coming from the chapel and had the good sense to save themselves.

I could not allow myself to contemplate what had transpired at Castle Cormoran until I was safely away. I rode Ianthe all the way to Leeds, where we both nearly collapsed.

I received plenty of stares as I walked, stiff and bloody, to the train station with a large brown horse in tow. I tethered her to a thick post and went into the washroom to try to clean myself up. I looked at my reflection in horror; I looked as though I had taken a blood bath. I tried my best to wash the blood from my face, hands, and hair, but it would not come out of my clothes, so I buttoned up the raincoat to cover the evidence. It wouldn't do to go walking around looking like I had just murdered someone. I was somewhat surprised to find Ianthe still tied up where I'd left her, and I reminded myself that this was not the United States. I untied her reins and stopped a man walking by with a suitcase.

"Excuse me, sir," I said, "but do you know where I might be able to sell a horse?"

He shook his head and moved on. I stopped several more people and asked them the same question; most of them looked at me as though I were crazy. Finally, I stopped a man who actually looked at the horse when I framed my question.

"As a matter of fact, miss, I own a stable myself."

I perked up. "Would you like to buy a horse?"

"She's a beauty." He looked Ianthe over, checking her teeth, her legs, the bottoms of her hooves. "How much do you want for her?"

"Anything," I said desperately.

"She's a fine horse...but I'm afraid I haven't enough—"

"How much do you have?" I blurted.

The man looked in his wallet. "Two hundred pounds."

"I'll take it."

"But—this horse is worth *much* more!" he protested.

"Look, mister, I don't have time to explain, but I have to get a train to London as soon as possible. I'll take whatever you'll give me for her, but I need cash, and I need it now."

The man seemed taken aback by my brusqueness, but obviously did not want such a good bargain to pass him by. He gave me the two hundred pounds, and I thanked him and ran for the ticket office.

It wasn't until I was on the train, headed for London, that I finally allowed myself to think about what I had done. My terror and my desire to put as much distance as possible between myself and Castle Cormoran had fuelled my escape all the way to Leeds; but now, my body finally allowed to rest on the comfortable train seat, my mind began to reflect on the whole awful nightmare, and I was overcome, to the point that I broke down into tears. I kept seeing that whole dreadful tableau: the blood that shot from Philip's body in great geysers; the flames that consumed Kieran, and all the horrible little creatures that had sprung from them; Eugenia's twisted, ravaged face. And through it all, I heard the bloodcurdling screams that I knew would haunt me for the rest of my life. But did I cry for Eugenia, for Philip, for Kieran—or for myself? Had I left a piece of myself behind, to be destroyed in the flames that claimed what was left of my family? I was now the sole remaining de Montfort, the sole remaining Ramsey. If I died childless, the family died with me.

I tried to close my eyes and sleep, but found this impossible. Before me, I kept seeing the flames rising higher and higher. How could I do such a thing? I heard Eugenia's voice shrieking my name, begging to be let out. Had I actually heard her, or was my mind playing tricks on me now? Was I a murderer? Was I now doomed to burn in hell, in a fire much hotter, much more nearly eternal than the awful blaze I had set?

***

Before leaving the United States, I had been excited about going to London. But now that I was there, I paid scant attention to my surroundings. I reserved a room at a small bed-and-breakfast hotel, and there I placed a long-distance call to my father.

"How's your trip going, sweetheart?" Dad asked, sounding as though he were anticipating tales of great adventures. I leant my head against the wall and closed my eyes. Hearing my father's voice seemed to put me back on solid ground for a moment, as though I were waking up from a bad dream. I couldn't possibly tell him what had really happened.

"Terrible. Dad…I can't explain it all now, but…I'm in London now, and I've lost my passport, my traveller's checks, my plane ticket—everything. I need you to get some money out of my savings account and wire it to me right away. And can you fax me a copy of my birth certificate or something? I have to get a new passport, so God only knows when I'll be able to leave here."

"How in hell did you manage to lose everything? Selena, for Pete's sake, can't you keep up with—"

"It's a long story, Dad, okay? And I'm not that negligent." I told him where to send the money and the fax before hanging up. I would have to buy some clothes and toiletries for the rest of my stay. There was too much to do, and I didn't feel up to any of it. I retired early that evening, shedding my bloodstained clothes to sleep in my underwear, my covers pulled tightly up under my chin for warmth.

I lay awake, mentally torturing myself. My parents had raised me a Catholic, but I hadn't been to church in years. It seemed strange, then, that I suddenly felt a need to go to confession—but what would I say? "I killed my family—they were vampires and ghouls"? Destroying a vampire wasn't considered a sin, anyway, was it? In the movies, *priests* were often called upon to rid people of the Undead pests. A man of the cloth, therefore, would applaud what I had done—if he even put any stock in it at all, in this rational, scientific age. So why did I feel so wretched? Because I feared the servants might have perished in the flames as well? No, I don't think that was the only reason.

Overcome by exhaustion, I finally dozed off into a fitful sleep, devoid of true rest. I saw myself lying in my own bed, back at home in my apartment, when I suddenly awoke to find someone standing over my bed. It was a man, his face and body horribly charred, almost beyond recognition; his clothes hung on him in blackened tatters, and his long hair was singed and ragged.

"Selena," he said accusingly, "how could you?"

I awoke with a small, strangled cry. As I realized that it was only a dream, my breath came in great gasps. I knew that voice well, whispering in my ear, bellowing out in rage, sending a tingle down my spine, a voice like no other…

Kieran's voice.

Chapter Eleven

The Book

I reported to the dining room the next morning for breakfast, having absolutely no appetite but realizing my body still needed food. I choked down actually very little of the large English breakfast and left the hotel to go pick up my money and buy some clothes. I tossed my old, bloody clothes into a garbage can and took a taxi to the U.S. Embassy in order to try to get a new passport. A Bach violin concerto seemed stuck in my head, playing itself over and over, seemingly without end. It was something I'd heard Kieran playing, and I tried to think of something else; but the music refused to go away, becoming louder and filling my brain. I felt as though I were going mad.

I tried to convince the people at the embassy that I needed to get out of England and back to the United States as soon as possible, but they appeared unmoved. They'd have it taken care of when they could, they said, but I had to go through all the necessary channels. I just wanted to get far away from England, to put the whole trip behind me. The violin concerto accompanied me back to my hotel.

I dropped off my things and left the hotel once again, to walk the streets, alone with my thoughts. Once again the weather was grey and dismal to match my mood, drizzling a fine mist on my bare head. Every stranger I passed had Kieran's face; every voice that cut through the heavy air was Kieran's voice. I felt a hand touch my cheek, a cold breath tickle the hairs on my neck, but no one was there. I reached a small, wooded park and sat down on a cast-iron bench.

I realized then that Philip had been a distraction, diverting me from that which I knew now to be the truth. The attraction I had felt to Kieran had been there from the start, from the first time I met him, but I hadn't realized it, had even fought it down. I hadn't trusted him; I had suspected ulterior motives in his dealings with me, and so I had tried to squelch the feelings that he stirred in me. Yet they had been there all along, from the moment he had first turned around and fixed me with that *stare*, those *eyes*. I didn't know how much to believe of Kieran's declaration that since he and I were more closely related (if one could even call it "close"), that we were the ones meant to be together. But I couldn't deny that there was something between us, something that transcended space and time. He had vowed to haunt me till my dying day, and it appeared that he was going to do just that. Perhaps we did share some sort of blood kinship; perhaps, in some dreadful way, we *were* alike. I hadn't wanted to face the evil desires that I knew lurked within me. I had spent all my life trying to force myself to believe that I was a "good" person, that evil had no hold over me. But now I could no longer ignore the war being fought inside me, inside my heart, my soul. I had drunk Kieran's blood, and now I would never be rid of him. But worse than that, I wouldn't have been able to bear it if I were.

***

I spent the rest of the day in the park; and when I got back to the hotel, I took a hot shower. I looked down and saw, to my horror, blood slowly running down my leg. I opened my mouth to scream, but then realization dawned on me: it was my menstrual period. I leant against the shower stall, crying with relief.

I dried off and returned to my room. I thought of my journal and felt again my irritation with Kieran for destroying it. He had been right about one thing, though—most of it *had* been about him. The old saying, "Truth is stranger than fiction," couldn't have been more apt. My old teen novels suddenly seemed empty, frivolous, devoid of meaning. I had the book of my career sitting in my lap, so to speak—every word of it true, not one word that would be believed. This was a story that was fairly screaming to be told, but I knew that the only way I would get away with it would be to change all the names and slap the label "Fiction" on it.

I had to remain in London while the whole mess with my passport was squared away, but I was unable to enjoy my stay the way that I had wanted to when I planned my trip. I checked the newspaper for a few days to see whether there would be any mention of a fire in an old castle in northern England, but there was none. I spent my days wandering aimlessly, becoming so hopelessly lost on more than one occasion that I had to call a taxi to rescue me and take me back to my hotel. I had trouble sleeping, and I spent many a night curled up on a couch in the public sitting room, vacantly watching the "telly." One evening a couple of Irishmen good-naturedly tried flirting with me; but I was not in the mood for any male attention, so I retired to my room, where I sat in the dark, staring out the window. I couldn't imagine anyone possibly being as miserable as I was then, unable to think of anything but Castle Cormoran and the inimitable Kieran Ramsey.

I couldn't help thinking of the contrasts Kieran presented, of the sweetness of his countenance as he lay sleeping in his coffin, or of the thought of him out riding with his young nephews. Such views of Kieran were hard to reconcile with the image of his hurling a dagger at Philip's retreating back or sending a platter of meat flying as he snarled at Jane. It made me wonder whether perhaps some shred of gentle feeling still lurked within the core of his being. Perhaps he had even been capable of love.

I knew such thoughts were sent to torment me. The thought of Kieran's possessing such a paradoxical personality seemed a vividly exciting possibility, much like the contrast between his refined looks and rough-around-the-edges voice. No mere mortal man I had known could have been nearly so charismatic. It seemed that Kieran's emotions, his very personality, had run always in the realm of passion, be it in one form or another. To spend one's life with such a man would undoubtedly be thrilling, though perhaps also exhausting and even frightening; but, like a heavily addictive drug, once one has experienced that rush, nothing weaker will do.

***

The trip back home seemed long and lonely. I put a tape into my Walkman, but the first thing that flowed into my ears was "Waltz of the Flowers," and I burst into tears. I was too embarrassed to look around and see how many people were staring at me.

When I stepped off the airplane in Atlanta and walked down the telescoping corridor into the airport, I found Valerie and my father waiting for me.

"Sel! What happened to you?" Valerie cried.

I stood woodenly as Valerie clasped me in a strangling hug. My father gently pulled her away and put his arms around me, as though I were his little girl again.

"Baby, what happened over there?" he asked, with a tenderness I hadn't heard in his voice in years.

"Oh, Dad, it was so awful—"

"What did those jerks do to you? I *knew* I smelled a rat."

"Dad, it's not what you think. I...I can't explain it." My father would have me in the mental ward at the hospital if I started babbling about vampires. "There was...a...a fire...I'm the only one who escaped."

Valerie looked horrified. "Oh, Sel, *no*!"

"I lost my passport and my plane ticket and my money and clothes in the fire."

"At least you're not hurt," my father said. I just looked at him miserably. *Is that all you think counts?* I said to myself. *I wish I were dead.* "I'm taking you girls out to dinner tonight," Dad went on.

"Oh, Dad, that's really sweet, but I'm just not hungry," I protested.

"You will be by tonight."

"I really don't think so, Dad—"

"Look, sweetheart, I know you've been through a terrible trauma, but it's *over*, you're *alive*, you have to get on with your *life*."

That's my dad: No time for tears. *Chin up, soldier!*

It wasn't until I got home and Rufus came running to greet me that I finally broke down. I scooped up his big, fuzzy body and wept into his soft fur.

"He really missed you, too," Valerie said. "I tried to bring him over to my place so he'd have some company, but Josh and Tabitha kept trying to beat up on him, so I brought him home. I made sure I played with him for a little while every day when I came over to feed him and clean his litterbox. He only coughed up one hairball, but I cleaned it up."

After Valerie left, I lay curled up on my bed with Rufus until my dad came to pick me up for dinner. He refused to take no for an answer when I said I didn't feel like going out, insisting that he had made reservations at my favorite restaurant.

I wasn't much company that evening. Valerie's prodding about my visit met with little more than noncommittal grunts and brief, almost rude, answers. I just wanted to go home and be alone. Valerie said she was going to check on me the next day.

I dropped off my film on the way home and immediately washed up and went to bed. I had the usual trouble falling asleep, and then when I did, I wasted no time in starting to dream. I opened the chapel door slowly, looking in horror at the piles of bloodless, decomposing bodies heaped disrespectfully on the marble floor. Dried bloodstains made most of the floor appear a dark, crusty red. On the floor in front of the altar, as though for a funeral, lay an open black lacquer coffin. I slowly approached it, afraid to look in but unable to resist. Kieran lay peacefully inside, looking as sweet and serene as he had that awful day when I had set him on fire. Slowly, he opened his eyes and fixed me with his hypnotic stare.

"Selena," he said, his voice very low, "drink my blood." He ripped open his shirt to reveal a wound over his heart—as though made by a stake—that suddenly began to gush forth great quantities of dark red blood. It splattered my face, my hair, the front of my clothes, as Kieran slowly reached out to grasp my arms and pull me into the coffin with him. He rolled over on top of me and we copulated there in the coffin's satin-lined interior as Kieran sank his teeth into my neck. I could feel my vitality being sucked out of me with my lifeblood, till suddenly Kieran reared back on his knees, tossing his head back. I saw then that he had two long, sharp fangs like a carnivorous animal and his mouth and chin were red with blood. With his eyes squeezed tightly shut, he let out a bloodcurdling howl that seemed to make his entire chest expand; and every one of the stained glass windows in the chapel shattered with a deafening crash. Tiny bits of colorful glass seemed to rain down on us, and one large, pointed shard hit me in the chest, imbedding itself in my heart.

I awoke with a gasp, clawing at my chest. I felt as though for a moment I had stopped breathing. I scarcely slept the rest of the night, and by morning my throat was raw and I was coughing up great hunks of mucous. My chest rattled with every wrenching cough.

Despite the fact that I was sick and had had little sleep, I was up early and reached the photo finisher's as soon as they opened. I was informed that my film was not ready, so I wandered the shopping center in a fog. The time passed with agonizing slowness, and I found myself unable to think of anything but the events that had unfolded at Cormoran. I felt unable to function, as though everything were in slow motion, and I was weighted down by some unseen force.

By the time I returned to the photo developer's, my film was ready. I paid for my pictures and opened the envelope with shaking hands. I leafed through picture after picture of the castle, inside as well as out, until I came upon the photo I had taken of Kieran's portrait. My eyes welled up with tears, and I put my hand to my mouth.

"Are you all right?" the young woman behind the counter asked, looking worried.

"Could I get an enlargement of this one, please?" I choked.

"Certainly." She brought me another envelope. "Just fill this out."

I filled out the envelope, placed the negative inside, and left with my pictures. I went home and sank down on my living room sofa, with the picture of Kieran. Was he truly going to haunt me for the rest of my life? Was this his revenge? Had I created my own hell by destroying the man I had desired more than any other, before our passion had reached its fulfillment? Or would hell have been my reward for giving in to him, trading my soul for the pleasure without end he could have given me, becoming like he was, immortal, subsisting on the blood of the living? Either way, I was damned.

I tucked Kieran's picture into the corner of the bulletin board above my desk and lurched to the sofa, where I collapsed. A moment later, there was a knock at the door. "Who is it?" I groaned.

"It's me, Valerie. Can I come in?"

I groaned again and launched myself from the sofa to shuffle to the front door. Valerie stood at my doorstep, regarding me with large, worried doe eyes. "How do you feel?" she asked.

"Rotten."

"What's wrong?" She followed me inside.

I sat down and let out a great, hacking cough.

"You have a cold," Valerie observed. "Or a sinus infection, or something."

"That wasn't what I meant." I collapsed into a fit of coughing, tears streaming down my face.

Valerie handed me a tissue. "You need to see a doctor."

I finished wiping my face with the tissue and turned to look at Valerie. She looked so worried—scared, almost. "I'm sorry I was a bitch last night," I said.

"You weren't a bitch. You're just suffering from post-traumatic stress disorder or something. It happens to a lot of people who've been through, like, big disasters." She walked over to the coat closet and removed a jacket. "Put this on. I'm taking you to the doctor."

"I don't want to go to the doctor."

"Well, you don't have a choice. You sound awful, Sel. I bet you have pneumonia."

It was useless to argue with Valerie, so I let her lead me to her car and drive me to a walk-in clinic. Stalwart Valerie stayed by my side in the waiting area, and she was still sitting there with that air of watchful protection when I came back out.

"What did the doctor say?" she asked the moment she saw me.

"Bronchitis."

"Did he give you a prescription?"

"They're calling it in right now."

Valerie looked relieved. "We'll pick it up on the way home."

I said little but coughed a lot on the way home. Valerie waited in the car while I went in to pick up my prescription, and she brought me home and ordered me to lie on the sofa while she made me some tea. I sat up and took the cup she offered me a few minutes later.

"Valerie," I said. "There's more...to what I said about the fire...something I didn't tell you."

Valerie sat down beside me. "What is it, Sel?"

I looked at her earnest face, and I knew I couldn't tell her—not the whole story, at least. But I felt I had to tell her at least *some* of it—as much as I thought she could handle—so that I might impress upon her a small amount of the anguish I was feeling. I took a deep breath. "I met someone over there."

Valerie's face lit up. "A *male* someone?"

"Yes. Very much so."

Valerie got a naughty twinkle in her eye. "I bet he has long hair."

"Yes."

"And he's British."

"Yes."

"Oh, Sel!" she squealed. "Tell me more."

"He perished in the fire."

Valerie's face fell. "No! That's *awful*!"

"Now do you understand why I'm upset?"

"Oh, Sel, how terrible! You mean you finally met your dream man, and then he *died*? Of all the rotten luck! And I bet you guys fell madly, passionately in love, too! Who was he?"

I smiled wryly at Valerie's "madly, passionately." It was useless to explain. "His name was Kieran Ramsey."

"*Ramsey?* You mean he was one of your *relatives* you went to meet? Isn't that sort of, um…*kinky*?"

"I believe it's only against the law with your *first* cousin, not one who's about fifty times removed."

"So, he was one of the castle dwellers, huh? I bet he was some sort of dashing, blue-blooded gentleman type. Am I right?"

"Sort of."

"That's tragic. You could have married him and lived happily ever after in your family castle. Do you have a picture of him?"

I knew I couldn't explain the portrait, so I responded with, "No. But I guarantee he was unlike anyone you've ever met."

"What did he look like? Was he handsome?"

"Very." I took a sip of tea and looked at Valerie's earnest face. Wistfulness and profound sadness competed for space on her countenance. She was such an open book. Dear, loyal Valerie. We had been best friends since high school. How could we not have been? We had always been so much alike. Like two peas in a pod, my mother used to say. When one of us started a sentence, the other would finish it. When one of us called, the other would say, "*I* was just going to call *you*." We used to joke that we were twins, separated at birth—except that we looked nothing alike. But now I feared that I was wrong all along. I was nothing like Valerie, whose motives were always pure and true. No, I knew now who my real twin was. We had even been born on the same day, though separated by four centuries. *We're two sides of the same coin, two halves of one soul. My blood is in your veins...and your blood is in mine.*

"Valerie," I said slowly, "there's something else I have to tell you."

"I'm listening."

I struggled with this for what seemed a very long moment before speaking again. Valerie waited patiently. "I...I'm the one responsible for the fire."

"Oh, Sel! But it was an *accident*!" There was no hesitation on her part. "You know it was!" She could not believe, even for a moment, that I was capable of anything so awful. Of course not. She still believed we were alike. I decided not to push it. I would never be able to make her understand. I started hacking again.

Valerie got up and walked over to my desk to grab a box of tissues. She spotted Kieran's picture and asked, "What's this?"

I tried to appear nonchalant. "Oh, that's a picture I took of a portrait at Cormoran."

Valerie leaned closer to get a better look, then turned and winked at me. "Looks like your kind of guy, Sel. Thin, long dark hair...and look at the expression on his face. He looks like somebody with a trick or two up his sleeve. He looks perfect for you. Too bad he was born a few hundred years too early. You must agree with me, or you wouldn't have stuck his picture up here—to give you inspiration? Am I right?"

"Cut it out," I said irritably, not wanting to admit how close she'd struck to home.

"Look, if there's anything I can do…you know, to help out…make you feel better…"

"I appreciate the offer, but there's nothing anyone can do."

Valerie took some convincing to get her to leave. Usually I enjoyed her company, but now I just wanted to be alone. All I could think of anymore was Kieran, and the bizarre turn my life had taken. I thought, perhaps, that writing about the whole sordid affair would not only allow me to wallow more deeply in my obsession with a certain black-haired, dark-eyed vampire, but that it might also serve as a sort of exorcism, a way of ridding myself of my emotional burden by putting it down on paper.

I sat at my computer and began working on my manuscript the rest of the day and well into the night, finally tumbling into bed, exhausted. But even sheer exhaustion was not enough to drive away the disturbing dreams. Kieran appeared to haunt me once again, to captivate me with his mesmerizing eyes and his seductive voice.

"Don't deny what you feel, Selena. I know you long to kiss my lips, to run your fingers through my hair…You cannot resist that, can you? I know you have always had a passion for long-haired men. Particularly men with long, *dark* hair. 'Tis your greatest weakness, is it not?" His coy little smirk told me he was enjoying this. "My hair is very long and very dark, and I think you shall find it very much to your liking. I think you shall also find my lovemaking very much to your liking…or you would have, had you not taken it upon yourself to destroy me. I could have made you immortal, my lady. Not only would you never grow old, never die, but you would have had me for your lover for all eternity. Do you know what that means, Selena?" He stepped closer and touched my face. "I was your dark angel, come to take you to Paradise. You cannot deny how I made you feel—so thrilled, so alive. You loved to hear me play, to dance in my arms, to watch me fencing or riding. You so loved to watch me, m'lady. I felt your eyes on me, eating me alive. But most of all, you loved my touch, my kiss. You would have loved to have all the rest of me as well. But you repaid my love with betrayal. You betrayed us all, Selena. Your own family." He removed his hand and gave me his dark, impenetrable stare. "And for that, m'lady, you shall never have peace…for as long as you live."

I woke up screaming. "Kieran! Why are you *doing* this to me? Haven't I suffered enough already?" I sat with my face buried in my knees, not wanting to admit that facing the rest of my life without Kieran was torture enough.

***

When Anne called to see whether I was back from vacation, I told her I was hard at work on my new novel—my first "adult" novel.

"Your vacation gave you some ideas?" she suggested.

"Yes. *Too* many."

"So—how were your relatives?"

"Let's just say—even I could never invent characters like that."

Anne laughed. "Well, I hope someday I get to meet them. But I suppose that's rather unlikely." *VERY unlikely,* I thought. "What's it about?"

"Let's just say it's a departure from my usual style. Oh—and, Anne?"

"Yes?"

"Let's drop the 'Young,' okay? I want this book to be by Selena Ramsey."

"Sure. You want a different name for your adult books than what you've used for your young adults, hmm? Where did you come up with 'Ramsey'?"

"It was my mother's maiden name."

"Oh, I see. Sort of a tribute to your mother?"

"Not really…it's just that…" My eyes slid to the photo of Kieran's portrait. "I'm coming to accept who I really am. I can't run away from it any more. There are some things you just can't run away from, and you can't fight."

I know Anne had no earthly idea what I was talking about, but she said, "Sure, Selena. That's no problem."

***

My bronchitis lingered for two and a half weeks before finally dissipating. Valerie took my cessation of coughing up phlegm as a sign that I was ready to go out and face the world. She insisted that I go with her to a classical concert, the reason, I'm sure, being that she thought I was spending an unhealthy amount of time holed up in my apartment. Truth be told, I was almost afraid to leave, and what happened that night was a good example why.

We did not find a close parking spot and had to walk several blocks. On the way, we passed several other people, and up ahead of us I saw a male figure dressed all in black, with long, almost straight, black hair that fell nearly to his waist. He appeared to be about average height, and rather thin. My heart seemed to have stopped. I blinked a couple of times, but he did not disappear. I ran after him, grabbing his arm and nearly spinning him around.

"What the hell?" a totally unfamiliar, very American-sounding voice demanded. As I looked at his face, I saw that he had a swarthy complexion and heavy eyebrows. From the front, he looked nothing like Kieran. In mortification, I released my grip on his arm.

"I'm sorry," I said, my voice sounding strange and faraway. "I thought you were someone else."

"Well, I'm not," he snapped, and walked away, mumbling, "Fucking crazy bitch."

Valerie caught up with me. "What happened?"

"He just...reminded me of someone. I freaked out."

"That guy you fell in love with? Sel, he's *dead.* He's not going to be out walking the streets of Atlanta."

Oh, the snappy comebacks I could employ if only I could have told anyone what had really happened. I let Valerie lead the way, and I numbly sat and tried to listen to the music and keep my mind from wandering.

Valerie had not told me what was on the bill for that evening's performance—a number of selections by Bach, including that which had been endlessly playing in my head and driving me crazy. One selection in particular had an alarming effect—the "Allegro assai" from Bach's "Violin Concerto in E." It sounded hauntingly familiar, and I remembered hearing Kieran play it for me. I sat staring at the violinist, unable to move. He seemed to slowly transform into Kieran before my eyes; then, the rest of the musicians and everyone else in the audience seemed to vanish, and the theatre shrank and turned into the music room at Cormoran. Kieran was playing only for me, his nimble fingers coaxing the sweet, soaring notes from his violin. I could see the tiny jerks of his head as he played, the graceful movement of his right arm with the bow, the coy little smile that framed his lips as he glanced at me from below the half-lowered lids of those hypnotic eyes. Then I was dancing in his arms, being swept across the floor as I wrapped my arms around him and held him tight, tangling my fingers in his hair, kissing him hungrily. This was followed by the shocking, arousing contact of skin against skin, lips against flesh, Kieran devouring me with his lovemaking, making me explode. I was suffocatingly hot, and dizzy, and everything around me was spinning wildly, so that I stood up, hoping to make my escape, but I was completely disoriented. I didn't know where I was or how I might get out, so I took the easy way out by blacking out and collapsing.

***

I became a sort of recluse after that embarrassing incident at the concert, afraid of anything that might remind me too strongly of Kieran. I devoted nearly all my time to my book and finished it in about a month. I sent it off to Anne but still remained holed up in my apartment, not wanting to go out and face the world.

Anne phoned me up after she'd had a chance to read the manuscript.

"I *love* it!" she cried. "Why did you never write horror before?"

"You think it's horror?" I asked, somewhat irked. "I thought it was more of…a love story."

"A horror/love story. A horror/romance. I think they used to call this sort of thing 'Gothic' or 'Gothic romance.' Yes, that's it. See, you can do it, Selena. I *knew* there was so much more in you. Wherever did you come up with something like this? That must have been *some* vacation. I guess there's nothing quite like an old castle to inspire a person."

"I suppose."

"These characters…I particularly liked the hero…or perhaps I should call him an 'anti-hero.' I can't really blame the heroine for falling for him; I think I did, myself, as I was reading it. Come to think of it, she sounds kind of like you. But then, I guess most of your heroines sound kind of like you, don't they? Selena, I honestly think this is the best thing you've ever written—so far."

Anne's enthusiasm for my manuscript must have been contagious, for she sold it to the first publisher to whom she submitted it. She even managed to talk them into trotting it out as quickly as possible and to procure my largest advance to date.

"I think you're on to something," she said.

I suppose I should have been happy—I was about to turn the most horrifying, depressing, and nerve-wracking event of my life into my most successful (and perhaps lucrative) work of my career. Yet I felt empty inside. Writing about my experiences had failed to exorcise my demons, and it would not drive away the dreams that still plagued me. Frequently they reminded me of that day when we had all been caught out in the rain. I would see Kieran standing shirtless in front of the parlor fireplace, just as I had on that day; but somehow, as he straightened up and flipped his long hair out of his face, I would realize with sudden horror that his hair was not damp with water, but with kerosene, as suddenly it burst into flame. And if I was not tormented by terrifying, guilt-ridden nightmares—with endless visions of bodies consumed by fire, the smells of burning flesh and hair, and the sounds of screaming and of Kieran's voice accusing me—then I was tantalized by dreams of Kieran's being my lover—sensuous, seductive, and dangerously exciting—so that I awoke weeping bitter tears of remorse and loss. As the time passed, Philip and Eugenia began to gradually fade from my dreams, but Kieran did not. He seemed to have gained a stranglehold on my subconscious, which he stubbornly refused to relinquish. So realistically did I experience his nightly visitations, just as I had at Castle Cormoran, that I began to wonder whether I had truly completed the job. Perhaps someone had saved him—one of the servants, or the dreadful black dog, Mephistopheles? What a name for a dog...what a sick of sense of humor Kieran had. Or perhaps the only reason I could find no peace was because I simply could not let Kieran go. I couldn't decide which possibility could be more frightening.

That I was unable to bury my dead—or perhaps, Undead—was obvious. The enlarged photograph of Kieran's portrait sat in a frame on my desk. Sometimes I just sat and stared at it for hours, my word processor's monitor blank, the cursor flashing incessantly, as though trying to tell me to get to work. Valerie often remarked on the picture when she came over on one of her frequent visits, as she tried in vain to get me to go to a party or allow myself to be fixed up with a blind date.

"What—mortal men aren't enough for you anymore?" she quipped.

"That's not funny," I snapped.

"Gee—excuse *me*! You know, you used to have a sense of *humor*, Sel. You used to be a fun person. I'm sorry you lost the love of your life in a fire, but, Sel, that was almost a *year* ago! You have *got* to get on with your *life*!"

"Look, just don't play psychiatrist with me, okay? You don't know the half of my problems."

"Sel, you do *not* have a corner on the market when it comes to suffering. Plenty of other people have been through what you're going through."

I eyed her exasperatedly. "I doubt that."

"Sel, *you* of all people should know about empathy. You're a *writer*, for crying out loud. It's your *job* to be able to empathize with people. Besides, you need to get out."

"I *am* getting out. I have my first autograph party for my new book on Thursday."

"Great! Am I invited?"

"I was hoping you'd come."

"I wouldn't miss it."

***

I liked to hold my first autograph signing for a new book at my favorite independent bookstore in Atlanta, a small shop in an older part of town. Although these affairs never seemed to be packed to the rafters, nevertheless, a respectable number of teenagers usually turned out for the occasion. When I arrived at the store that night, a number of teenagers had already gathered there, along with a few college students. I could tell it might take a while for people to catch onto the fact that this was not another of my teen novels, but I knew some of these young people were "regulars," and I was grateful for their support.

Valerie sat next to me at the table after she had gotten the readers to form a neat line. After hearing several people tell me that they were my biggest fan, I began to notice a change in the people lining up for autographs. There were young people, obviously younger than I, wearing black leather, combat boots, or old Victorian clothing, people with hair dyed black and faces painted white. One fellow even had "*Le Non Mort*" painted on the back of his black leather motorcycle jacket in white letters, with a red blood drip beneath.

"Where did these people *come* from?" Valerie whispered in my ear. "Somebody tell them it's not Halloween."

"When did you start writing horror fiction?" a girl in a tiny black mini skirt and silver snake earrings asked. "I just *love* vampires."

"I've already read your book, and it is *so* cool," said another. "Are you going to write horror from now on?"

"I *loved* it! You write like you were really there."

I tried to accept my fans' compliments with grace and poise, even though I had the creepy feeling of being caught in a bad dream, trapped in some bizarre underworld from which I could find no escape. Without exception, the young people had all been extremely polite and appreciative, yet I could not shake the feeling that I was being watched from the shadows, eyed by someone with evil designs upon me. The group finally dispersed, leaving behind only a few customers browsing amongst the books.

"I'm going to run to the bathroom," Valerie said.

I felt as though I were on the verge of an anxiety attack. "Don't go," I burst out.

Valerie was rising to her feet, and she gave me a funny look. "What's the matter, Sel? You'll be okay. Can't I even go to the *bathroom*? I'll be right back."

I nervously watched Valerie disappear into the back room. I looked at my watch. I had another half hour to go.

"Ms. Young—er, Ramsey?" a voice asked, making me jump. I turned to see the assistant store manager standing to my left with a stack of my books. "Could I get you to sign these to put on the shelf?"

"Oh—sure," I said distractedly. She set them down and walked away. I began to sign the books, my hand shaking slightly, when suddenly I became aware of a presence. At about the same moment, out of the corner of my eye, I saw two hands come to rest on the table in front of me. I shifted my gaze to look at the hands without moving my head; they were masculine hands, smooth and fair-skinned, with long, slender fingers. My heart seemed to stop for a moment and then to pound frantically, as an icy tingle went down my spine and my legs went numb. I recognized those hands. I had seen them gripping a sword, holding the reins of a fierce black horse, coaxing sweet music from a violin—and I had felt them touch me. I slowly looked up, into the mesmerizing dark eyes that had haunted all my sleeping and waking hours for nearly a year.

Kieran stood before me in all his magnificence, showing no sign of the scorching he'd received. Not even the ends of his hair were singed. He leant over the table, so that his face was only inches from mine. I felt that surely my heart had stopped this time, and I couldn't seem to breathe. He fixed me with his hypnotic stare, and I couldn't have looked away if I wanted to.

"You're quite handy with a shovel, m'lady," he said, his voice scarcely more than a raspy whisper, "but I'm afraid you missed one."

About the Author

Ria Dimitra was born and raised in Huntsville, Alabama, although she has also resided in Minneapolis, St. Paul, and Nashville. *The Blood Waltz*, her first published novel, arose from a fascination with vampires that began in high school, a love of Gothic romantic fiction, and a solo trip to England.